I0521458

Finding the Way to Your Heart

Marcie Shumway

A New Reality Publishing
South Paris, Maine

Finding the Way to Your Heart. First Edition.

Published by A New Reality Publishing, 54 High Street, South Paris, ME, 04281.

Visit our website, www.ANewRealityPublishing.com, for more information on other *Reality: It's All In Your Mind*™ materials and to view the full line of our books and products.

Copyright © by Marcie Shumway, 2016.

Cover design and book layout by Christopher S. Harris, A New Reality Publishing.

Original cover photography by Jessica Woodcock, Lost in Reverie Photography

Manufactured in the United States of America. All rights reserved. No part of this book may be reproduced in any form or by any electronic or mechanical means, including information storage and retrieval systems, without permission in writing from the publisher, except by a reviewer, who may quote brief passages in a review.

ISBN 0-692-71768-4
ISBN13 978-0-692-71768-4

Table of Contents

Finding the Way to Your Heart
Marcie Shumway

<u>Dedication</u>

"Grandmas hold our tiny hands for just a little while, but our hearts forever."

For my Grammie ~ I love you

Acknowledgements

First and foremost, I want to thank my amazing husband. None of this would have been possible without him, his support, and his love. On the days I have questioned this journey he has kept me on the path I have truly wanted to follow.

I also need to thank my wonderful editor, Jennifer Harris, and my publishing company, A New Reality Publishing and the owner, Christopher Harris. These characters would still be waiting to tell their stories if it wasn't for you. Your support and help through this entire process is greatly appreciated.

Lastly, a huge and special thank you to Jessica Woodcock of Lost in Reverie Photography. Her beautiful photos cover the book, much like the last one. I never would have guessed our partnership would turn into the friendship it has. However, those that are passionate in life do tend to find each other.

About the Author

Marcie Shumway has been writing short stories for others to enjoy since she was in middle school. Finding the Way to Your Heart is the second book she has published. She is an avid reader that thrives on the many books of her favorite authors.

Marcie resides in a small town in Maine with her loving husband. The two share their home with their cat, Kyzer, and their dog, Dani. They also have two horses, Chance and Dee.

<u>Chapter 1</u>

The bedroom door opened with a creak. I pulled the blankets tighter around me and squeezed my eyes shut hoping that it would close again. I felt him move to the side of the bed and it shifted as he sat down beside me. His hand came down on top of my head and smoothed my hair back down. I willed my breathing to stay regular so that he would think I was still sleeping. The next thing I knew the blankets were pulled away from me...

I sat straight up in bed trying to shake the dream, I didn't have to finish it to know what happened next. Tears were streaming down my face and the tank top and shorts I had worn to bed were plastered to my body with sweat. I looked up and turned off the alarm clock when I saw that it read 4:30 AM. It wasn't worth it to try to go back to sleep for another half hour.

I rolled out of bed grabbing my workout clothes from the dresser on my way by, along with my cell phone. After a quick clean up in the bathroom and a change of clothes, I was stretching and making my way to the living room. I refilled the wood stove that had burned all night. The house was still warm, but there was a definite chill in the air. There was something to be said for the beauty of a Maine winter, however the temperatures left something to be desired. I finished the task and grabbed my boots. As I laced them up I looked around.

The cabin was about 1,200 square feet. It was all one level and only had one bedroom with a master bath. The kitchen, dining room, and living room were an open floor plan which was great when someone wanted to entertain. The woman I rented from was amazing and I couldn't have asked for any better. Straight out of high school I had been itching to get out of the house while I attended community college. Susan Crow had been Bob Hunter's bookkeeper at Hunter's Rig Repair and she had purchased the little plot of land from him. The cabin had been built just for her. When JJ, Bob's son, had taken over the business I had mentioned my interest in helping out in the office. Susan offered one better. Not only did I take over her position in the office, she offered me her house to rent so she could spend time in Florida.

    I grabbed my gym bag from the floor by the couch, and my keys from the bowl by the door before heading out to the attached garage. When I opened the garage door a blast of cold air hit me and I was grateful the gym wasn't more than a few minutes away. The jacket and boots I wore worked to protect me from the cold weather, but definitely not the workout pants. With cold air blowing through the vents of my 2008 Jeep Grand Cherokee Laredo and 90s Pop blaring through the speakers I made the quick trip to the local gym, and was relieved to find only one other vehicle in the lot ahead of mine.

    I slipped into the locker room to change my shoes, remove my jacket, and lock up my bag. As I made my way out to the main room of the building where all the equipment was, I slipped my iPod into my arm band and the earbuds into my ears. Hopping onto an elliptical I set it for mountain terrain and got moving. The warm up at the beginning gave me a chance to admire my workout "buddy", it was the whole reason I had chosen this machine. It had a view of the entire room, including the weights.

Chad Conrad was a beautiful specimen of a man. Clad in athletic shorts, sneakers, and a loose tank top, most of his muscles were clearly visible as he squatted. His striking blue eyes met mine in the mirror and he favored me with a small smile and a nod of the head. I smiled in return and felt my cheeks get warm at having been caught checking him out. However, with the view in front me it was hard not to. He was well toned between the gym and the outdoor work that he did, yet he wasn't completely muscle bound. He was just right inside and out by most women's standards. Unfortunately, I didn't stand a chance with him.

The machine I was on switched gears and I turned my attention to the task at hand. A half hour into the workout I think I had finally burned off the nightmare that had gotten me up extra early. Sweat dripped down my face and as I brought my towel down from wiping it off, I found Chad leaning on the elliptical next to mine nursing a water. I felt my face instantly warm again under his gaze as the machine moved to cool down mode.

"Good morning sunshine," he greeted with another of his dazzling smiles.

"Good morning handsome," I returned the same way I always did, despite the butterflies in my stomach.

Now it was his turn to blush. Chad had always been shy and timid, even with his good looks. He was someone that was willing to give the shirt off his back for anyone and was forever being approached by women, yet I could probably count on one hand the number of dates he had been on since high school. He was a great catch if any woman could reel him in.

Just as the machine ended its cycle, and I stepped down beside Chad, the door opened and we were joined by another couple. Skye and JJ Hunter, the newlyweds, came in on a gush of frigid air. They both glowed with happiness and who could blame them. After years of being apart they were reunited and even with things standing in their way they were together, married, and expecting their first child in the spring. The two kissed and made their way to the locker rooms to change, waving excitedly at us when they passed by.

"I guess I'll head out," I murmured grabbing my towel from behind me.

"You don't have to bail, Lisa, just because they're here," Chad said halting my movement with a hand on my arm.

"I'm not."

"You are," he replied with a reassuring smile. "It will get easier."

I smiled in return and headed back towards the locker rooms, passing Skye on the way. I sat on the bench in front of my locker and rested my head in my hands. Even though everyone thought I was in love with JJ and that I disliked Skye, it was actually the opposite. I was excited and happy for them. They proved love could conquer all. Sure, I had taken advantage of his pain years ago and had tried on more than one occasion to get him to look at me the way he looked at her, but it wasn't because I loved him. It was because I wanted a shot at what they had, yet didn't feel like I deserved it. The real man I wanted, and had been in love with for years, deserved so much more than what I could give him and thought of me as nothing more than one of the crew. Maybe it was time to pack up and start over.

Chapter 2

The phone was ringing off the hook the moment I stepped foot into my office that morning. Between anxious customers waiting for their sleds to be done, delayed parts orders, and sick workers, my morning was a whirlwind. To make matters worse, my cell phone was blowing up. My mother had felt today, after six months of no communication, was the day to catch up.

After getting off the phone with a vendor that assured me our parts would be delivered that day, when they were already two days late, I put my head down on my desk with a thud. Taking a few deep breaths, I closed my eyes and attempted to calm down before I threw something across the room. I definitely wanted to go back to bed and start the day over.

"Rough day?"

My head snapped up at Chad's voice. He stood in the doorway holding two to-go bags from The Pit, my favorite local restaurant and pub, and a travel tray with two drinks. Looking at him a second too long, I couldn't decide if he looked better in his gym clothes or his Carhartt's and work boots, I nodded.

"Nothing seems to be going right," I told him as I closed the vendor file on my desk and laced my fingers together over it. "You just missed JJ, he ran away to have lunch with his wife."

"I know," he responded entering the room and setting everything down on the table in the corner.

I raised my eyebrows at him as he shrugged out of his Conrad's Cabins & Lodge beanie and his Carhartt jacket. Once the layers came off he proceeded to unpack lunch. When he was done he turned around and closed the door. As I got up from my desk to deter him, given the craziness of the day, my phone rang. I sighed. Reaching for it with the greeting on my lips, a large warm hand came down on mine to stop it.

"A half hour. No phone, no customers, just us eating. You need a break."

"Thanks, but JJ..."

"But JJ nothing," Chad cut me off. "I already talked to him. After this morning I figured you could use a pick-me-up, and he said it hadn't gotten any better since you got here."

"I give," I said chuckling and gently pulled my hand out from under his.

Sitting down at the table I noticed for the first time what he had brought me. A BLT on toasted wheat bread with seasoned steak fries and a strawberry shake. My favorite meal from the restaurant. I was taken back. How did he know my order?

I looked at him questioningly, but he just smiled and gestured for me to eat. The conversation was light and was about everything except work, mostly friends and his family. If only I could keep him for myself, I thought as he told me a story about some of his family's latest guests at the cabins. If only it could be like this all the time. Chad always knew just what to do and say to make me feel better.

"So, how's your mom?" He asked leaning back in his chair signaling he was done eating.

14

I groaned and stuck my straw in my mouth, hoping that it would end the direction of the conversation. I knew Chad wanted to know why my phone was vibrating across my desk, and why I had muttered about her just mere minutes before. I didn't exactly know myself since I hadn't answered the phone or messages, but I had had a pretty good idea. His eyebrows came up and he chuckled because he knew I was avoiding it. I just wanted to stay in my perfect little lunch bubble, and she wasn't invited.

Before I could respond, my door swung open and Will, an older gentleman that worked the front counter, stepped in "Hey Lisa, we have two customers out here, one with questions on an invoice and the other looking for some ball joints that I can't seem to put my hands on."

I quickly grabbed the trash from our lunch and dumped it in the trashcan by the door. I knew exactly who they were so I went around the backside of my desk to grab the files I had waiting, and started to make my way out.

"Thanks for lunch, Chad," I told him as I leaned back into the door frame in my haste to get out front.

"You're welcome," he replied pulling his jacket back on.

"We will talk about this!" was the last comment I heard as I walked out. I didn't want to think about that conversation. I wanted to continue on in my content haze brought on by a sweet lunch. My family and our problems had no room in my brain at that moment.

"How are you today, Mr. Erikson?"

<u>Chapter 3</u>

It hadn't been easy, but I had somehow managed to avoid the topic of my mother. Both JJ and Chad seemed to know that something was off with me, and that it had to do with her. When they couldn't get any information out of me they even had gone so far as to send in Skye and Sam, another member of our rat pack, to coerce me into lunch and gossip. Unfortunately, instead of leaning on all of them like I knew I could and should, I continued to withdraw. It was getting harder and harder to keep all my family secrets bottled up inside.

It was Friday night, thankfully, and with Christmas a week away and a fairly large snowstorm heading towards Maine, I was ready to hibernate alone for a few days. I had taken one look in the mirror after work and when I saw the dark circles under my hazel eyes and the listlessness of my shoulder length brown hair, I decided it was time to slow down and practice some self-care. It was also time to make the phone call I had been dreading. I was on the couch wrapped in a fleece blanket with the TV on a Hallmark Christmas movie and my cell phone in my hand. It was now or never.

"Hello?" came my mother's tentative reply when she answered the phone.

"Hi mom," I greeted albeit with some fake cheer and my retail voice.

"Oh baby! I've been trying to get ahold of you!" she exclaimed.

"I know," I told her, pinching the bridge of my nose between my thumb and fore finger. "We've been a little busy at work." At least it wasn't a complete lie.

"I'm sure you have. JJ is very good at what he does."

I mumbled a response and waited. I knew there had to be a reason behind her phone calls. She went on to talk about my stepfather, Craig, who was an absolute sweetheart and definitely would have been my choice for her after my father had died, and my stepbrother, James, who I could have cared less about. Then I heard the ball drop.

"You're what?!" I asked to make sure I had heard her correctly.

"Craig and I are coming to Birch Wood for Christmas and New Year's. We've already booked a cabin with Karen and Duncan at Conrad's," she informed me happily.

"That's...great," I forced out as panic welled up inside me. "Mom, I've got to go. Text me the details. Love you."

I immediately felt guilty for getting off the phone so quickly, I couldn't hold back my tears any longer. I felt like everything was crashing down around me. How was I going to handle them being here for a few weeks? I couldn't even handle a half hour telephone conversation with her. I didn't know how much longer I could keep everything inside. I curled into a ball on my side and let years of pent up emotions come spilling out. The sleep I needed would have to wait.

The next day I didn't come-to until almost noon time. I felt drained, yet lighter all at the same time.

Dragging myself from the couch I made my way to the master bath and set the shower water as hot as I could tolerate it. I spent the next half hour letting water wash away my tears from the prior night, and trying to feel somewhat human again.

While I was pulling on clean yoga pants and an old Hunter's Rig Repair sweatshirt I heard someone pounding their boots off on the porch, and then letting themselves in. I wasn't too worried because I knew only a handful of people had a key, or knew where I kept the spare. I dried my hair a little more with the towel and looked at myself in the mirror. My hair was a bit of a mess, but looked better than it had the night before. My eyes, on the other hand, were now red and puffy instead of sporting the dark circles. Shrugging at myself, I dumped my laundry in the hamper by the door and made my way out to see who my visitor was.

I found Chad in the kitchen in his stocking feet and clean work clothes, unpacking what looked to be homemade soup. Noticing his layers of clothes, jacket, and boots by the door, I grabbed them and put them near the woodstove to dry out. I looked up and saw that the storm had started earlier than predicted and several inches of snow already covered the ground. Making my way back to the kitchen I figured I would help Chad.

"Is your mom trying to fatten me up again?" I asked laughing since it was a long-standing joke that she and Duncan thought Skye and I were too thin.

"She worries," he stated turning around with a smile, which faded quickly when he saw my face.

I knew it was bad, but I hadn't thought it was that bad. Now I was reconsidering not having put on any make-up. He approached me, concern in his eyes, and cupped my face with his hands. I gasped from the combination of the contact and the chill.

"What happened?" he asked quietly wiping away imaginary tears with his thumbs.

I leaned into his touch and covered his hands with mine. Oh this sweet man. If only I could be so lucky as to get to keep him. Closing my eyes, I shook my head and felt real tears slip through my eyelids. I felt his lips whisper across mine in the briefest and sweetest of kisses.

"I'm here if you need me," he told me simply as he kissed my forehead and stepped away to finish with lunch.

Oh wow! While I watched him set the table I just stood there, frozen. What did that kiss mean? Was it just a friend to a friend? Did he REALLY care about me? No, it wasn't possible. I wasn't gorgeous like he deserved, or even that smart. He could find so much better. We were just really good friends and he was a caring guy...right?

Chapter 4

The soup and the company was just what I needed on this stormy day, especially after the emotional toll of the night before. We ate in silence, but it wasn't awkward. No questions were asked. I didn't know if I should be on edge because Chad might start pushing for answers, or if I should just relax and let things happen as they did. When we finished the meal I shooed him away so I could clean up since he had brought everything over.

I expected him to bundle back up to head out, however as I washed dishes and put them in the strainer I could hear him turning on the TV and getting settled on the couch. Finishing up, I turned around and chuckled when I found him engrossed in one of my favorite Hallmark Christmas movies. He waved his hand to quiet me only causing me to laugh harder. I received a mock glare and a pillow for my efforts.

As I headed over to the couch to join him I realized he was smack in the middle. Before I could contemplate any further, he tugged on my hand and brought me down directly beside him. Chad shifted and put his arm around me on the back of the couch, tucking me against his side. As much as I wanted to snuggle into him and take in the smells that were his alone, I was confused.

"I don't bite," he whispered in my ear.

"Never thought you did," I teased back, "though I may have hoped you would a few times."

The smiled from him was quick and caused him to pull me closer into the crook of his arm. Flirting I knew, but

I worried about messing up my friendship with him if things went too far. It could never be long-term between us, and JJ and Chad had always been there for me. After a few moments of his fingers drawing delicious circles on my shoulder and bicep I gave in. I relaxed into him and nestled into his side.

Between Chad's warm body pressed against mine, with his hand rubbing circles on my back where it had moved to on its own accord, the storm outside, and the TV playing low I was lulled into a relaxed and nap like state. I was aware of the movie ending and another starting, not much else. A few hours later I woke up, startled when he dropped the remote on the wood floor. I had somehow changed position and was now laying down on top of Chad as he laid on the couch.

I didn't move a muscle. The feelings I and his body were having, didn't feel very friend like. What was going on? I wasn't good enough for him. Didn't he know that? I continued to "sleep" as I felt him shift to check something on his cell phone. What was I supposed to do?

"You can stop playing possum," Chad finally murmured.

I peeked up at him and found him watching me with a soft smile playing on his lips. His left arm was behind his head as a second pillow and his right was against the couch beside my body. I couldn't help but melt a little and smile back. Every woman wanted a man to look at her the way he was looking at me.

Feeling his fingers start to rub circles at my hip through my pants, I scrambled up. Too fast, evidently, as I immediately had to reach out to steady myself. Chad never moved, except to raise his eye brow at me in

21

question. I shook my head as I stumbled around the furniture. He was just too inviting.

"Bathroom," I muttered moving quickly to the bedroom and the master bath.

I closed the door behind me, and took a deep breath. When I looked in the mirror I startled myself. My hair was sticking up at all angles and my cheeks were flushed. I grabbed my brush and tamed my hair into a short ponytail. Splashing cold water on my face I took a couple more deep breaths. My mind was spinning. I wiped off the excess water and opened the door to head back to the living room. I couldn't hide forever.

Chad stood by the door pulling on his jacket. He had already put on his boots and his other layers of clothes. I stood back, leaning against the arm of the couch to watch him get ready to go back out into the storm. He motioned for me to come closer before he put his gloves on. Hesitantly I went to him.

"I have to go open up driveways," he told me taking my face in his hands, "I will be back, with supper."

"You don't need to."

"I know I don't *need* to. I *want* to," he emphasized leaning towards me.

I was so stunned I stood motionless as his lips brushed over mine in another sweet kiss. I opened my eyes slowly while giving him an inquisitive look. He just smiled leaning in to kiss me again. My eyes fluttered closed. This time his lips caressed mine gently and he took his time before pulling away. Chills ran up my body.

"What was that?" I whispered.

"If you don't know," Chad chuckled, "I'm doing it wrong."

"That's not what I meant," I said, my voice louder this time, and my eyes opening the rest of the way.

"I don't want to just be your friend anymore."

As he said that he pulled on his gloves, opened the door, and headed out into the snow. Had I just heard him right? Did he just basically say he wanted me as his girlfriend? I backed up and sat on the arm of the couch and watched him clean out the driveway and leave. Now I was even more confused.

<u>Chapter 5</u>

It was after dark before I heard Chad's truck reach the driveway. He dropped his plow and the lack of noise alerted me that the snow was still coming down at a good clip. I had changed the TV to Friends and had the fire stoked when he finally came in, shaking off at the door. I reached for the to-go bags from The Pit and proceeded to unpack supper while he pulled off his layers of clothes.

"How much is out there?" I asked setting the table with paper plates and plastic ware.

"Right now it looks like almost eight inches and they are calling for another eight or so before morning," he answered putting all his stuff by the woodstove to dry.

I shuttered with an invisible chill as I looked out the kitchen window into the darkness. I hated snow storms. I knew I was safe and warm where I was, but the idea of getting snowed in made me nervous. Lost in my own thoughts I was startled when Chad came up behind me and wrapped his arms around my waist, nuzzling into my neck and lightly nipping. I sank into him. It was what I had wanted for so long and despite my heart warming with the idea of us as a couple, my head was screaming with warning bells.

"Have you thought about what I told you before I left?"

"How could I not?" I retorted with a snicker as I turned out of his arms and head back to the table with the remaining food in my hands.

He didn't miss a beat with my answer and dug into the refrigerator for drinks. He set a water down in front of me and poured himself a glass of milk before sitting down next to me at the table. We started eating and I wondered if he was just going to let the whole thing go. The chicken and mash potatoes were mostly gone and I had just grabbed a knife to cut us each a slice from the small chocolate cream pie that had been included in the bag, when he finally spoke up.

"Are you going to talk to me?"

"I don't know what you want me to say, Chad," I said, frustration creeping into my voice. "You tell me you don't want to just be my friend anymore. So, does that mean that if I just want to be friends that I'll lose your friendship? I don't know what to think."

"You know that's not the case, Lisa," he stated patiently.

"Do I?"

"I'm not going anywhere, no matter what you tell me your feelings are. I have been here this long haven't I?"

"What does that mean? When exactly did these feeling start?"

"Years ago," he told me simply.

I sat his plate in front of him with the pie and just stared at him. Years ago? Where had I been? I tried to rack my brain for any indication that he had felt that way. We had flirted and teased, but I had always been careful about keeping it light and friendly. He and JJ had always been my saviors when I needed anything, from help with lawn work to plowing, and anything in between. There was one thing that he and I had in common that no one else did though, something special.

"You can't tell me that you don't feel the same way," he said breaking into my train of thought.

"You deserve better than me," I whispered starting to pick at the pie on my plate.

"Well, at least that's not a no," he responded softly, while reaching over to grab my hand I had laying on the table.

"You should have a beautiful woman that is adventurous and enjoys all the things you do. Someone that isn't broken like me," I informed him, tears welling up in my eyes.

"Look at me, darlin'," he requested lifting my chin with his fingers.

I brought my eyes up to meet his and my heart soared. His blue eyes were warm and caring, his smile easy and all for me. I couldn't hold in the tears any longer. Chad didn't need my secrets weighing him down too. The sobs came next. Before I could protest, he was picking me up and carrying me to the couch. He sat down, putting me on his lap and wrapping me in his arms.

The tears were short lived as I soaked up his strength. My heart was still wanting this to work so badly, but my head was telling me I was not good enough for him. I shifted to put my feet on the couch and changed my angle so that I could rest my head on his broad shoulder. He leaned his cheek against the top of my head and took one of my hands in his, intertwining our fingers.

"You are beautiful, adventurous, and not broken. As for enjoying all the things that I do, you and I have never had a problem spending time together."

"Chad, there is so much you don't know about me."

"So, we learn about each other. That's what people do in a relationship."

He said it so matter-of-factly that I had a hard time arguing. I sat up and turned slightly to look at him. He had a five o'clock shadow that just increased his good looks. His blonde hair was short as always and I rubbed my free hand over it and down his cheek. Silently he leaned into my hand and turned his head to kiss my palm. I closed my eyes and sighed, then opened them again to find him studying me.

"We don't need to rush anything," he whispered, "but I want the chance to at least try to make it work."

I leaned down and met his lips with mine. This time I was in charge of the kiss so I kicked it up a notch and ran my tongue along the seam of his lips seeking entrance. He moaned quietly and opened slightly. Our tongues met and tangled gently. His grip on me never changed and remained light. I could feel the tension building as we continued the kiss so I pulled away.

"Okay, I give."

Chad smiled at me and picked me up to unceremoniously drop me back on the couch. He then handed me the remote and went to clean up the supper mess still in the kitchen. I found a Big Bang Theory marathon and figured we could both use the laughs so I left it there while I grabbed a fleece blanket from the recliner on the other side of the living room.

I was just settling back down when Chad came and sat down next to me. We both put our feet up on the coffee table and wrapped the blanket around our legs. Snuggling into his side much like I had earlier in the day with his arm around my shoulder pulling me close, I couldn't help but be happy. The heck with what my brain thought was right. At this moment, with the smell of this magnificent man surrounding me and his warmth seeping into me, I was going to be happy and go with my heart.

<u>Chapter 6</u>

I awoke to the sun pouring over me. I did not want to get up. I felt so warm, safe, and cocooned next to Chad, and I just wanted to stay there forever. Then I felt the bed move and my eyes opened, reality setting in. It wasn't my bed that was moving, per se. I had slept all night on the couch on top of Chad, much like I had napped the day before.

The sky was as blue as it could be, which meant today was clean up and Chad needed to get moving. I basked in the warmth a few minutes more before I tried to quietly untangle myself. I figured he could sleep a little longer while I made him breakfast. However, my attempts were thwarted when I felt hands clasp onto my waist to keep me from moving.

"You keep wiggling like that and you'll find yourself in a different position real quick," Chad growled.

I grinned to myself and peaked up at him. His eyes were still closed, a smile gracing his lips. I rolled my hips for good measure and broke free quickly before he could get a better hold. I heard him groan in good natured frustration as I headed for the kitchen.

Humming and smiling to myself I bopped around the kitchen preparing waffles and bacon for breakfast. I wanted some comfort food and it was something that would stick with him for a while as he plowed. The bacon was in the oven and the first batch of waffles in the iron when I finally saw Chad pad his way to the master bath. I set the table with syrup, juice, and butter, and was so caught up in my own world that I bumped solidly into Chad's chest when I turned back around.

"I could get use to this," Chad stated as he wrapped his arms around me.

"The morning cuddling or the food?" I asked arching an eyebrow.

"Both," he replied, "and this."

Before I could pull away he had my cheek cupped in one hand and his lips were coming down on mine. It started as a sweet brushing of lips, however, there seemed to be some undercurrent of electricity with us because after a few quick brushes our mouths and tongues collided and dueled. The hand that had been cupping my cheek slid to the nape of my neck to change the angle of the kiss, and his other hand slid down my back and hovered just above my ass. I dug my nails into his t-shirt, bunching it at his shoulders and ground my hips into his. His groan and the feeling of his arousal on my belly snapped me back to reality.

I pulled away slightly and he easily released me, giving me a quick pat on the rear before turning to grab the plates and silverware on the counter. I eased around him to take the waffles out of the iron and to add fresh batter. Moving beside me he pulled the bacon from the oven, and using a fork moved it to the plate covered in paper towels I had left out. I tried to gage his mood as we worked flawlessly around each other to finish making breakfast. I didn't want to deter him from touching me, but at the same time I didn't want us to rush it. He seemed content enough though, despite my breaking away from him earlier, as he hummed and smiled.

Sitting down to eat fifteen minutes later we were still quiet. I wasn't sure exactly what to say or do. Chad smiled fully at me from across the table after he took a sip of his juice and covered one of my hands with his giving it a squeeze.

"We'll take it slow," he reiterated, "though I may catch pneumonia from the cold showers I am going to have to take."

I chuckled squeezing his hand back and started to eat heartily. Suddenly my appetite was back. We finished our meal in silence, yet it was comfortable. It felt like we were a little old married couple. The ease that we moved around each other in the kitchen was consoling. The light brushes against each other and the murmured conversation we shared filled my heart.

"You going to let me come back?" he asked pinning me with his arms on either side of me as I leaned against the sink.

"Maybe," I teased crossing my arms over my chest.

"Please," he begged leaning in to nibble on my neck.

"Keep doing that and I'll think about it," I told him giggling and sighing all at once.

He proceeded to trail slow sweet kisses from my ear down to my neck. I uncrossed my arms and set them on his hips. I could definitely get used to having him around and the affection he showered on me. Suddenly my cell phone went off, startling us both.

Not paying attention, I grabbed it and answered. It was my mother. She was talking so fast I almost couldn't understand her. I pulled away from Chad while I listened to her go on about the cabin that she and Craig were staying in. Evidently they had come in the night before, in the middle of the storm and they had just gotten up. She was saying something about getting together as I wandered to the living room. Chad was there putting on his layers to head out.

"Mom, hold on a minute," I cut her off so I could say good-bye to Chad.

"I'll text you later?" he asked pulling on his hat and leaning towards me to drop a quick chaste kiss on my lips.

I nodded touching his face before he pulled away. I needed his strength and comfort more now than he knew. He kissed my palm and pulled on his gloves, waving slightly as he made his way out the door. I watched him clean up the deck through the window as my mom continued chatting in my ear.

I hoped I could do this. I needed to juggle my family and Chad. I could do it. The secret would stay with me and everyone would be fine. Who was I kidding? I was going to go crazy while they were here. As for Chad, this would never work. I had to tell him that we were better off as friends.

<u>Chapter 7</u>

I texted Chad after getting off the phone with my mother and told him not to come back and that I didn't think us in a relationship was going to work. Tears were streaming down my face as I sent him another one explaining that I didn't want to lose his friendship and that I cared about him deeply. I knew that I was chickening out by texting him, but doing it face to face would just be too hard for me.

I spent the rest of the day cleaning the house, knowing I would have company in the next day or two, and packing my gym bag for the next morning. My mind was so full of stuff that sitting wasn't an option and when I tried to get to sleep it was a long time coming and fitful. Not to mention my dreams were filled with Chad and my dreaded secrets.

BEEP! BEEP! BEEP!

I slammed my hand down on the alarm clock and rolled over. It couldn't be 4:30 already. It felt like I had just gotten to sleep. I rolled back over and sure enough 4:35 AM glared back at me. Grumbling I climbed out of bed and got ready to go to the gym.

As I pulled into the parking lot a half hour later I groaned out loud. I had half hoped Chad would skip the gym that morning after my text message. I hadn't heard back from him, so I assumed he was upset and hurt. That alone had sent me into another round of tears. Again we were the only ones there, at least I didn't need to worry about anyone else noticing the awkwardness between us.

Finding the Way to Your Heart
Marcie Shumway

Somehow I made it into the gym, geared up in the locker room, and out to my machine without ever connecting with him. My peripheral vision assured me he was there though, doing free weight arm exercises. As tempted as I was to watch those muscles ripple as he worked out, I just couldn't. I put my ear buds in, focused straight ahead, and got lost in my own little world.

The next thing I knew I was covered in sweat and my routine was over. I shook my head and got off the machine. The room was completely empty. I cooled down and stretched, suddenly feeling very sad. Obviously I had ruined everything with Chad, including our friendship. He had never left the gym without saying goodbye before.

Grabbing my towel from the machine, I wiped my face and made my way to the locker room. My muscles were mush and my brain still on screech. I wasn't sure what to do about my mom and Craig, nor was I sure what to do about Chad. I was just outside the door to the women's side of the locker room when I was spun around and pinned in the corner of the hallway by a strong, solid body.

"You're lucky I don't know karate or something," I teased.

I had known it was Chad before he even had me against the wall. His smell was engrained in my memory. His arms were on either side of my head, his hands braced on the wall, and his body was inches from mine. The heat from his workout was still radiating off him.

"I think I can handle you," he said, his voice low and sending chills down my spine.

I looked up and found something in his eyes I didn't expect, determination. The lust from both of us was evident, but I didn't see the hurt I thought I would. Swiftly a thrill ran through me. Maybe I hadn't ruined things as badly as I thought.

"I hate to tell you this," he smirked. "It will take more than a text message to get rid of me."

Oh boy, I had severely underestimated the quiet, sweet Chad I knew. This was another side of the man, and damn if I didn't like it. I ran my hand up his left arm to his bicep where his tattoo was. It was of an empty hunting tree stand at sunset with a cap hanging from it. It was a replica of the one his grandfather used to wear. At the base of the tree above the dates of his grandfather's life, and his initials was a single rose, a rose that matched the one on my hip. I had wanted a tattoo at eighteen more than anything and Chad had agreed to go with me. I had been pleasantly surprised when he had gotten one as well and had incorporated mine into his own. That was the day I had realized I was in love with him.

"We can make this work, I'm always here for you," he whispered leaning down to kiss me gently.

I took the hand that rested on his bicep and snaked it up his shoulder and around the back of his neck. Pulling firmly, I brought his lips back down to mine and took control. He kept his hands where they were on the wall, but he opened his mouth and allowed me the access I was seeking with my tongue. The kiss was hot and full of lust. Finally, I pulled away, leaving us both panting.

"I'm doing what's best for you," I whispered back before ducking under his arm and going in the door behind him.

I leaned against my locker for a good five minutes before I was able to stop shaking enough to get dressed.

Finding the Way to Your Heart
Marcie Shumway

Chad must have left right after our altercation because when I made it to the parking lot his truck was gone. I felt my phone vibrate in my jacket pocket as I started my Jeep, so while I waited for it to warm up I checked my messages. One was from my mother...

Have a surprise for you! Can't wait to see you!

I hated surprises. Sighing I moved to the next one, which was from Chad...

You are what's best for me <3

Chapter 8

Trying to drive back to the cabin was tricky as tears were again streaming down my face. It seemed like I was doing an awful lot of crying lately and I wasn't a crier under normal circumstances. This man was going to cause me to purchase stock in Kleenex. Could I be lucky enough to have him as my boyfriend? I was broken, whether he believed it or not.

When I pulled in the driveway I was met with what I assumed was my mother's surprise. There was a newer Chevy Equinox in the driveway with Massachusetts plates that I could only guess was theirs and my porch was completely decorated for Christmas. Little white lights and garland were wrapped around the posts and the railings.

I pulled my Jeep into the garage and once I had it in park I put my forehead on the steering wheel. I needed to compose myself before I went in otherwise I would get badgered with questions. I wiped my tears with the sleeve of my jacket and took a couple of deep breaths. Just as I was gathering my things from the passenger seat I heard the door to the garage open. Bracing myself I jumped out.

"My baby!"

"Hi, momma," I greeted as she hugged me.

Despite all my reservations, I had to admit it felt good to have my mother's arms around me. When she stepped back to look me over I inspected her as well. Her cheeks were pink with happiness and she seemed to have a never-ending smile. She was in good shape and the jeans she wore were tucked into stylish calf high boots. My mom had had me when she was eighteen so she was younger than most of my friend's mothers. She sported a hooded sweatshirt from Hunter's Rig Repair that was probably mine and she could have easily passed for my sister rather than the woman that had given birth to me.

"You look amazing, Lisa," she told me honestly as she wiped the tracks the tears had left on my cheeks.

"Oh mom," I cried, breaking down again.

Putting her arm around my shoulders she steered me into the house. She only left my side long enough to shoo Craig into the kitchen and to grab a cold wash cloth. Curling us both up on the couch with a fleece blanket she cradled me and wiped my tears, much like she had when I was a child. I was lulled into a daze as she played with my hair and my tears slowed.

"I called JJ before you got here and asked if you could have the day off to spend with us. I hope you don't mind."

"Nope, I think we are long overdue for a visit," I admitted closing my eyes and soaking in her touch and scent.

"Do you want to talk to me and tell me what that was all about?"

I shook my head and opened my eyes, that's when I noticed it. They had taken over my cabin. I suddenly wasn't so relaxed. They had not only decorated my front porch, but had also gone hog wild in the cabin. There was a small bare Christmas tree that I could only assume we were going to trim together, there were also ribbons and garland everywhere. It smelled wonderful, don't get me wrong, but I had stopped celebrating the holidays a long time ago. It hadn't been a fun, joyous time of year for me after we lost my father.

"What is up with all the decorations?" I asked sitting up and straightening my hair.

"I thought it would be nice to celebrate Christmas here this year, together," she stated waving for Craig to join us. "You can't have the holidays without the decorations."

My head started to swim. Clearly my mom's overbearing nature had not gotten better with age. Things always had to be her way. She was a wonderful mother, don't get me wrong. Nurturing, loving, but also very strict. We lost my father to a drunk driver when I was eight and it had only gotten worse without him there as a buffer. I was incredibly grateful that she met Craig two years later. He had been my savior during my teen years.

"Mom, you really didn't need to do this," I started, "we have been invited to the Conrad's."

"Nope. I talked to Karen and we will eat with them Christmas Eve, but we will celebrate Christmas here together and that is that."

I looked to Craig for some support, he just shrugged his shoulders as though to say "You know how your mom is". I leaned back on the couch and closed my eyes. I really was happy that they were here, yet a lot of time with them in a small confined space was not a good thing. How was I supposed to keep my secret? Of all people, they couldn't find out. It would crush them.

I allowed myself to be conned into decorating the tree for the rest of the morning while we listened to Christmas music and reminisced about years past. I had to admit it was warm and comforting. Craig still showered my mother with love and watching the two of them made me a bit jealous. I wanted what they had. Unfortunately, it wasn't meant to be for me.

When we were done we went to The Pit for lunch. By then I was ready for a nap and to have my house to myself. My mom was constantly asking about my love life and Craig was teasing me. You would have thought I was a teenager rather than in my mid-twenties. We were about to sit down when I heard a familiar voice from behind us.

"Why don't you sit with us?" Duncan Conrad asked again.

"Of course!" my mother gushed turning towards the table he was occupying with his son.

I rolled my eyes at Chad as Duncan greeted my parents. He smiled and winked at me before hugging them himself. Duncan came around and hugged me as well and kissed me on the cheek.

"When are you going to leave my son and run away with me?" he teased pulling the empty chair beside Chad.

"When you decide you want to leave Karen," I teased back.

"Dad, really?" Chad chuckled sitting back down.

The meal went surprising well and fast. I forgot how well my mother and stepfather fit in with everyone around Birch Wood. People were constantly stopping by to chat with them, and Duncan. Chad and I sat back and took it all in. I loved listening to them tell stories about their high school days, especially when they included my father.

"How 'bout dinner tomorrow night?" Chad whispered in my ear as his father argued good naturedly with Craig about who was paying the bill.

"I thought I told you we couldn't do this."

"I thought I told you, you can't get rid of me that easily," he retorted nuzzling the side of my neck gently.

My insides turned to mush and the familiar tingles he invoked in me came to the surface. Clearly he couldn't see that he could do better than me. Maybe I should show him. However, I valued our friendship too much. I was scared I would lose him altogether. Yet, if he didn't stop the nuzzling or move his hand that was running up my leg to grip my inner thigh under the table, I wasn't going to be able to say no.

"Fine," I finally caved, stilling his hand with my own.

"Good. I'll be there at 6:30 with the fixings for spaghetti and meatballs," he told me squeezing lightly with one hand and handing the waitress his debit card with the other.

I laughed at his antics considering our parents were still arguing about it. He smiled and his blue eyes lit up. I couldn't help it and leaned over to kiss him lightly, touching his cheek as I pulled away. The surprised look on his face was priceless, as was the sudden silence from the other side of the table. Oh boy, this was going to take some getting used to.

<u>Chapter 9</u>

"What to wear? What to wear?" I muttered to myself the next evening.

I had been home an hour and more than half of my wardrobe was spewed across my bed. I knew it was only Chad, but a girl likes to feel pretty when she spends time with the man she loves. It was still hard for me to believe that we were actually going to try this relationship thing. The little voices in my head kept telling me he deserved better, yet my heart was bursting. I had sent a couple more texts to try and deter him, in my panic moments, however the responses were enough to keep my heart on the winning side.

I finally settled on a pair of skinny jeans, a hunter green V-neck long sleeve, and wool socks. I quickly threw everything else back in my closet knowing that if he needed to use the bathroom he would have to walk past my bed. Some things you just didn't need to see that early in a relationship. Chuckling, I brushed some color on my cheeks and put on light lip gloss. Inspecting myself in the mirror I fluffed my straightened hair one more time and headed out of the bathroom and towards the living room.

I heard someone at the front door and it swung open just as I reached the woodstove. It was Chad, early, and laden with grocery bags. I moved to help him, he waved me off as he shed his boots before traipsing towards the kitchen with his treasures. Turning, I squatted to stock the woodstove. I had barely closed the door, and moved to stand up when large hands circled my waist and lips came crashing down on mine.

The heat behind that kiss was filled with lust and emotion. Our tongues tangled for control and our hearts pounded. As his hands slid from my hips around to cup my ass and pull me tighter against his arousal, I moaned into his mouth and hopped to wrap my legs around his waist. This brought us core to core and elicited a moan that came from Chad this time. He moved us to the short hallway and braced my back against the wall. I rocked my hips into his a couple of times and felt the pressure building and my panties getting damp.

Chad pulled away slightly and slowed the pace. He moved his hands up my sides and around to cup my breasts through my shirt, flickering his thumbs against my nipples. His eyes never left mine. I moaned softly and rocked against him again. Our mouths reconnected, his tongue caressing mine, this time gently circling and teasing.

KNOCK! KNOCK!

"Lisa! Are you home?!" my mom hollered through the door.

Chad and I pulled our lips apart and rested our foreheads against each other's. We were panting slightly and I could feel our cores still hot and pressed together. His manhood twitched and he growled low enough that only I could hear. Closing my eyes, I leaned my head back against the wall and took a couple of deep breaths. He moved his hands to cup my ass once more, and to help steady me as I untangled my legs and let them drop to the floor.

"I can't find the key!" she hollered again, jiggling the door knob. "Is everyone okay?"

"I'll be right there," I assured her raising my eyebrow at Chad.

"I feel like I am back in high school," he muttered smirking and shrugging his shoulder at my questioning look.

I ran my fingers through my hair on my way to the door and straightened my clothes, though I'm pretty sure that my mother would take one look at my flushed cheeks and know exactly what we had been doing. Internally I was grateful Chad had locked the door behind him and not put the key back as things could have gotten awkward real fast, yet I wondered what would have happened if visitors hadn't shown up. Smoothing my shirt one last time I turned to check with Chad and found him nowhere to be seen. Poor guy, I thought giggling to myself, and opened the door.

"It's about time. I was worried and it's cold out here," my mother blustered, her arms full of grocery bags and Craig right behind her.

"Well it's nice to see you too," I commented dryly. "What are you guys doing here?"

"We ran into Chad at the grocery store and he mentioned he was coming here for dinner, so we thought we would join you," she told me setting her bags down next to his on the table and shedding her jacket into Craig's waiting arms.

"You just thought you would join us?" I asked dumb founded.

She nodded like it was a stupid question and went about unpacking the bags. I looked at Chad, who had returned and was standing in the hallway, he put his hands up in surrender and shook his head. I spun my head around to look up at my stepfather, who had come up beside me, and he just smiled and put his arm around my shoulders to give me a squeeze. I put my arm around his waist and squeezed back, shaking my head.

"Fine," I relented. "What can we do to help?"

An hour later we were all seated around the table with steaming plates of spaghetti and meatballs. Garlic bread sat in the center of the table warm and sliced as well. Most of the conversation was about things that happened with our rag tag group of friends while we were in school, and where everyone was at now. It was wonderful. It was light-hearted and filled with laughter. I finally started to relax and enjoy the fact that my mother and step-father were visiting. These were the times that made the overbearing side of her easier to tolerate.

"I'm so glad you two finally got together," my mother commented gesturing towards Chad and myself.

"She hasn't exactly made it easy," Chad teased bumping legs with me under the table.

I felt my face flush and I took a sip of my wine to help me swallow the garlic bread I had been eating. I saw the look on my mother's face and inwardly I cringed. I knew this conversation wasn't headed in a good direction.

"I don't understand," she said looking at me and putting down her silverware.

"I do," Chad told her leaning back and draping his arm around the back of my chair to run his fingers lightly up and down my side.

"She has had a crush on you since the day we moved here," she started as I shook my head to stop her.

"Mom, I was five," I protested.

"Still, you told me that first day of school you would marry him," she continued, "and every time I saw you two together from then through high school, you looked at him the same way I used to look at your daddy."

Chad looked at me with a caring smile and a raised eyebrow. His fingers kept rubbing small circles to try to comfort me because he knew I was upset. Some might think this little information was funny and that someday we would look back at this and laugh, but right now it was stirring up memories of my secret. The one that I kept hidden from everyone, including my family. How was I going to do this for another few weeks?

<u>Chapter 10</u>

I made record time getting to the gym the next day. I woke up just as fired up as I had gone to bed, well if you can actually wake up when you don't really go to sleep. I had tossed and turned all night.

After we had finished dinner Craig had somehow convinced my mother to leave. Chad had stuck around and cuddled with me on the couch, watching a movie and trying to comfort me against the demons he knew nothing about. However, my secret was slowly taking its toll on me.

Opening the door of my Jeep, I was happy to see that no one else was around. I would have the whole place to myself, at least for a little while. Grabbing my bag, I made my way inside and quickly got ready in the locker room. With my iPod in place I went out to an open spot on the floor and did some stretches. When my muscles felt lax and warm, I jumped on the nearest treadmill. Today was about running out my emotions.

The slow jog I started with didn't take long before it was a full blown run. Metallica pounded in my ears in beat with my feet hitting the mat. Sweat started to drip, but instead of my mind clearing, it started to race. My nightmares flashed through my head, the secret I held inside me was clawing to come out. As the machine slowed to cool down mode, I stumbled, barely catching myself before I face planted. Tears blurred my vision.

Climbing off the machine, I swiped at my eyes to clear them and ripped the buds from my ears. My legs gave out between the two treadmills and I hit the floor hard with a thud. Sobs wretched from my body so deep and so hard it physically hurt. Small strong arms wrapped around me and I leaned into the comfort, not caring at that moment who it was. That's when I felt the baby bump and knew exactly who was holding me.

I'm not sure how long we sat there wrapped around each other. The tears eventually slowed and the sobbing finally stopped, though I had a huge ache deep in my chest. I pulled away and took the towel she offered to mop up my face. Skye helped me to my feet and led me to the locker room. Once there, she pointed towards the benches while she grabbed one of the towels the gym provided and wet it down with cold water. Handing it to me, she sat down beside me.

"Did JJ or Chad ever tell you about Steve and I's relationship?"

I shook my head, unsure where she was headed with this conversation. She rubbed her belly with a small glowing smile. I saw tears fill her eyes and I reached for one of her hands. Fingers interlaced she started talking again.

"Steve started getting physically abusive right after I graduated from college. It gradually got worse each time. The last time it happened, he strangled me until I almost blacked out...and he raped me."

My mouth dropped open. I couldn't form any words. This woman I had secretly admired and been jealous of for years, was just as broken as I was. Only she wasn't really broken, I realized. She was beautiful, in love, and growing rounder each day with her first child. Skye was even more amazing than I originally thought, yet she was just like me.

"I was sexually abused by my stepbrother. It started when I was ten, right after our parents got married, and lasted until I was fourteen. He is four years older than I am and at the time threatened my life and my mother's if I ever told anyone. To this day, she and Craig don't know."

Now was her turn to be speechless. She looked at me with tears streaming down her cheeks, still holding one of my hands while the other rubbed her belly. I felt like a weight had been lifted. Physically and emotionally, I felt lighter.

"That's why you did what you did with JJ and why you keep pulling away from Chad?" she asked wiping her face.

"Yeah," I said letting out a breath, "It wasn't ever about JJ at all. It was about wanting what you two had. Chad, well, he deserves better."

"Oh, Lisa! You are beautiful, strong, and loving. He couldn't do any better."

"It's very sweet of you to say that, considering everything," I told her, letting go of her hand to get up and stretch my tightening muscles.

"I mean it," she said getting up as well and stopping my movements with her hand on my arm. "Let him love you, help you heal, and love him in return. You *deserve* it."

Before I could argue with her, she pulled out her cell phone and showed me a picture. I brought my hand up to cover my mouth in shock. It was Skye, or at least it looked like her, with bruises along her cheek, a swollen shut eye, and a hand print around her neck. Tears threatened to start again until I looked up and saw the fire in her eyes.

"That was me on my worst day, that was the day I decided I was coming home to the people I loved. Getting JJ in the end was an added bonus."

With that she picked up her gym bad and her jacket to head out the door. This time my hand on her arm stilled her movements. Her eyes softened as she gave me a few seconds to compose myself.

"Thank you, Skye," I told her giving her a smile and her arm a squeeze. "I needed that more than you will ever know."

"I'm always here," she replied covering my hand with her own and squeezing back. "Trust him enough to tell him. Let him love you and help you. He won't let you down."

This time I let her go. With a final wave and smile she was gone. I splashed water on my face to clean up the tears and sweat then freshened up before heading out myself. The parking lot was starting to fill with the early birds and I was very grateful that I had been extra early so that Skye was the only one to witness my breakdown.

My thoughts kept straying back to Chad as I pulled out onto the main road to head home. I agreed with Skye, he would never let me down and would support me. The question was, how much did I want to lean on him? Would he be turned off by my secret? Those thoughts had me on autopilot obviously because the next thing I knew I was parked in front of the lodge at the Conrad's. I sent JJ a quick text to let him know I would be late and pulled my jacket tighter around me before getting out.

Chad would be in the barn feeding and grooming the few horses they kept year round, so I immediately went there. As soon as I opened the door and stepped in, the comforting smell of horse and hay filled my nostrils. I sighed and made my way down the alley to where I could hear Chad humming along to the Lady Antebellum song playing on the barn radio. The animals were all out in the paddock enjoying this beautiful winter day and he was obviously getting a head start on evening chores.

When I found the stall he was in, he had his back to me spreading sawdust, so I leaned on the door and took him in. He had shed his jacket and wore a black long sleeved Conrad's Cabins & Lodge shirt and his customary beanie with his Carhartt pants. The muscles moving beneath his shirt and his low baritone voice humming sent chills down my spine.

"Hey you," he greeted, finally catching me out of the corner of his eye.

"Hey back," I replied on a sigh, finally relaxing for the first time in who knows how long.

My sigh had him turning fully around to face me. My eyes must have been puffy from all the crying and my face streaked with tear tracks because he immediately put down the fork he had been using and approached me. Wiping his hands on his pants briskly, he then brought them up to cup my face and ran his thumbs across my cheeks. I covered his hands with my own and smiled at him.

"Everything okay?" Chad asked, worry etched in his face.

"Getting better every day," I answered stepping closer and getting on my tiptoes to kiss him. "Getting better every day."

Chapter 11

Christmas Eve dawned cloudy and threatening, but it didn't damper my spirits one bit. For the first time in years I was excited for the holiday and happy to be spending it with family. A little forecasted snowstorm was not going to hinder my plans for the day, after all, we lived in Maine. Snow was a given.

Instead of going to the gym, I allowed myself to lounge around in bed for an extra hour. Burrowing deeper under the covers I looked around and realized something. I had absolutely no pictures of my friends and family. Come to think of it, I didn't have any in the living room either. My secret had always kept me feeling alone and unattached. That was going to change!

Popping out of bed I put on workout clothes and commenced to cleaning every square inch of the cabin. My mother and Craig would be spending Christmas Day here with me, and with any luck Chad would be here a good portion of the day as well. With the tree lights twinkling and *Rockin' Around The Christmas Tree* blaring I danced around. Life was feeling pretty good.

A few hours later, the cabin was finally up to par. I checked the clock and found that I still had plenty of time before Chad came to pick me up. My family and I would be spending the evening at the Conrad's for their yearly Christmas Eve party. The difference this year was that I was looking forward to it.

Lathering on lotion when I got out of the shower, I heard Chad come in the front door. He was early as always and was whistling some Christmas tune. Despite the fact that the bedroom door was closed, my body reacted to his presence. My nipples hardened under my red lace bra and I could feel heat pooling in my matching red thong.

Turning my thoughts elsewhere before I got carried away, I pulled on my jeans and the red low cut baby doll top. It was conservative enough for a holiday party, but would give my cleavage some show time as well. I had picked it out strictly to catch someone's attention. Once I was dressed I opened the door and returned to the bathroom to finish getting ready. I had just finished my make-up when I heard Chad coming through the bedroom, and then a low whistle.

"Keep your hands to yourself, Cowboy," I teased putting my hands up when I saw the look in his eyes.

"Just. One. Kiss."

"Nope," I said brushing past him quickly to grab my socks and boots. "Save it for later."

The look on his face was priceless and had been just what I had been aiming for. When I got up from putting on my cowboy boots I gave him a chaste kiss and pulled him from the bedroom. I didn't waste any time closing up the stove, grabbing my present for the Chinese auction, and putting on my jacket. I knew if we stayed too long sparks would ignite and we would never make it to the party.

The snow had started coming down while I was getting ready, obviously, because a new coating covered the ground and crunched under my boots as we made our way to his truck. As soon as we were on the main road headed towards the lodge, Chad reached for my hand, interlocking our fingers and brushed a kiss across the back of it. Tingles shot up my arm and I squeezed his hand in return. When he turned his attention back to the road I took in his profile. Freshly cut, his hair was in a buzz cut, more for convenience than anything else, and it took on a dirty blonde hue in the winter. His blue eyes were sparkling and happy, and his strong jaw was relaxed with the ghost of a smile dancing on his lips. I wasn't sure exactly what I had done to deserve this gorgeous man, but I was ever so grateful.

Pulling into the Conrad's I noticed the vehicles of some of the guys from Hunter's Rig Repair. JJ must have invited them. My heart swelled with love for both my blood and non-blood family. Chad gave my hand one final squeeze before releasing it to turn off the truck, and come around to open my door. I turned in the seat as he opened it and allowed him to place his hands on my hips to help me down. He made sure our bodies brushed as my feet touched the ground and he planted a sweet kiss on the end of my nose. Smiling up at him through the snow I didn't think I could love him anymore than I did at that moment.

"Okay, kids," a voice rang out, "either get in here or get a room."

JJ stood at the entrance of the lodge grinning. I rolled my eyes at him as I stepped around Chad, allowing him to close the truck door. Skye came up beside him, smacking him in the chest for his teasing, and engulfed me in a hug the minute I stepped onto the porch. I hugged her back for all I was worth eliciting large eyes from both of the men. I smacked JJ on the chest as well on our way by him to go into the house and just smiled.

"What is up with these women?" he muttered rubbing his chest dramatically and earning a chuckle from Chad.

Chapter 12

The party was lively and wonderful. Any customers renting cabins were there, including a couple families with young children, the employees from Hunter's Rig Repair, the Conrad's, my mother and stepfather, and of course JJ and Skye. After a couple of hours of socializing and games, I snuck away with a plate of veggies and dip to sit down and take a breather. I loved to people watch. My parents were engaged in an animated conversation with the Conrad's that made me smile. I really wanted them to start visiting more, they just fit here.

Moving my gaze across the room I saw Chad talking with JJ, with Skye nearby. That man alone made my smile grow. Suddenly I saw Skye grab Chad's hand and put it to her belly. Baby Hunter must have been kicking. I watched the emotions flicker across his face, from surprise to wonderment to warmth. I had never thought much about kids, but seeing Chad look at his adopted sister that way, made me want to give that to him. Well, that was something to think about.

Focusing back on my plate I nibbled a bit and pondered. I realized that we were missing two members of our rag tag group. Kyle and Sam didn't seem to be in attendance. I looked around the room one more time and, sure enough, they weren't. Feeling a weight sit down next to me I turned my head to find Skye beside me.

"Are Kyle and Sam not coming?" I asked leaning around her to toss my plate in the nearest trash can.

"Nope," she replied snatching some of the remaining veggies before my plate hit the can. "They have been kind of distant lately. I'm not sure what's going on."

"You're right," I acknowledged, trying to remember the last real conversation I had had with Sam, other than when her and Skye had taken me to lunch not long ago. She had even seemed off that day come to think of it.

"Ever since our wedding," Skye voiced. "They ended up going to visit his parents in Florida, I guess."

Before we could talk more about it, Chad's mother, Karen, ushered us all into the large living room for the Chinese auction. The family like atmosphere and the good natured competitiveness kept it quite entertaining. I ended up with a moose figurine dressed in fishing gear and a $ 25 gift card for Doc's Donuts, so I really couldn't complain. After the gifts were done we moved to the dining room which was set for a family style meal that Karen, Skye, and Morgan, Chad's sister, had spent the day preparing. Other than the look I was getting from Morgan, it was perfect. Clearly she had heard about Chad and myself and did not approve.

When dinner was over some people visited a bit longer, but most left due to the storm. The roads were becoming snow covered and slippery according to Duncan. I wasn't too concerned since Chad was driving and he didn't seem to be in a hurry, so I helped Karen and Morgan to clean up. Carrying some of the serving platters from the dining room table, I went into the kitchen where Karen was busy washing those dishes that couldn't go in the dishwasher.

"It was a great party as always," I told her cleaning small amounts of remaining food off the plates into the trashcan. "Thank you for inviting me and my family."

"I'm so glad you could all come," she responded from behind me. "It is especially nice knowing my son is happy and loved."

I froze. It wasn't a secret Chad and I were together, yet I guess I hadn't realized that I had worn my heart on my sleeve. I always tried so hard not to put my feelings out there for everyone to see. I turned around slowly to hand her the dish and she gave me a warm smile.

"Chad would never intentionally hurt you," she said taking the platter from me and after setting it down, taking my hands in hers. "He is a caring, loving man."

"He is your son," I half teased tightening my grip on her hands.

"This is true," she chuckled, "but I see him with people. He cares openly and loves deeply when he does."

"Which is exactly why she doesn't deserve him," cut in a sharp voice from behind.

I looked over my shoulder at Karen's gasp and found Morgan in the kitchen doorway. The two of us had always struggled to get along and it had just gotten worse when Skye had come home. It made me sad to hear the harsh tone of her voice. I heard Karen's tongue cluck in disapproval and when I turned all the way around to face Morgan I saw Chad behind her. He was definitely angry.

"No," I replied moving towards her to go through the door, "I don't deserve him."

I brushed past her grabbing Chad's arm on the way by. I didn't want him fighting his family for me. I wasn't going to come between them, and he and Morgan had always been close. He finally relented putting his arm around my shoulders to pull me close while we walked to grab our jackets and kissed me on the forehead before releasing me. Silently we dressed to head out into the storm.

"I'm so sorry, Lisa."

I shook my head at Karen and gave her a hug letting her know that it wasn't her fault and I didn't hold it against her. I was afraid that if I said anything I would break down. Chad gave his mother a hug as well and ushered me outside and to his truck. Obviously either Chad or JJ had come out prior to start it, and clean it off. We climbed inside and made the trek to my cabin, still in silence.

When we pulled into the driveway Chad made quick work of plowing it out. Before I could get out of the truck, he jumped out and shoveled a path to the deck. He then cleaned off the deck enough so that we wouldn't track inside. I could see the controlled anger rolling off him still from his sister's comment.

Coming back to open my door for me, I climbed out and followed him to the house. He took my key from me and let us in. We took off our boots, gloves, and jackets all without saying a word. I was starting to worry that this night was not going to have a good ending when I was suddenly pinned to the wall by Chad's solid body.

"You do deserve me," he ground out, tipping my chin up with his finger so we were eye to eye. "You are a strong, beautiful woman and I love you. I don't care what my sister thinks."

Before I could utter a word his mouth came crashing down on mine. While his tongue danced around mine, I slid my hands up his abs loving the feeling of his muscles dancing beneath his shirt and over his defined pecs. Bracing myself for a moment on his shoulders I nipped at his lower lip and earned a deep growl from him in return. His hands came around my ass to pick me up and press my core to his growing erection. This time the moan came from me as I wrapped my legs tightly around him and dug my finger nails into his back through his shirt. Suddenly, Chad stopped and put his head against mine. His breathing coming in shallow spirts.

"Stay with me tonight," I whispered, moving my head to nuzzle against his neck and leave a trail of kiss up to his ear.

"Are you sure?" he asked pulling away to look me in the eye.

I rocked my pelvis against his suggestively and grabbed the back of his head with one of my hands to pull his mouth back to mine. Gripping me tightly with one hand around my waist he somehow locked the door and maneuvered us to my bedroom. Putting me down on the bed, Chad reached over his head and pulled his shirt over it. I gasped at the play of muscle on his arms, pecs, and abs. He wasn't as lean as JJ, but damn was he a gorgeous specimen of a man and all solid muscle. I sat up and undid the button of his pants and his zipper before he could react. Smiling, his blue eyes dancing in the light of the lamp I had left on, he shucked his pants and leaned down to pull my shirt off over my head. Now was my turn to grin, as he stood there taking in the red lace bra with just enough push-up to make it look like the girls were going to come falling out at any moment. I undid my own pants and shimmied them down my legs. The thong caught his attention as well and drew his touch. He ran his fingers over the lace on my inner leg brushing under it ever so slightly to tease.

"I'm not sure if I should take my time or if I should just ravish you," he told me forcing me back onto the bed as he crawled between my legs.

His hands made their way up my sides making trails of goosebumps along my skin. His mouth left open mouthed kisses from my belly button up to the cleavage I was sporting. Dipping his tongue between my breasts he reached around quickly to unclip my bra before pulling it off and latching onto a nipple. I moaned coming off the bed to meet his hips with mine. His suckling had me quickly wetting my panties as I brought my hands up to hold him to my chest. Wrapping my legs around his waist and locking my ankles at his lower back I rocked hard a couple of times.

That was all that he needed. Pulling my thong down my legs as he got off the bed I writhed in anticipation. Chad removed his boxer briefs and his member sprang free, hard and throbbing, my eyes were drawn to it while I watched him roll on a condom I wasn't even aware that he had. The minute his first knee hit the bed I was reaching for him. His hands came up to grip mine above my head and he latched onto the other nipple as he entered me in one quick thrust. He tried desperately to focus on suckling and to slow the pace, but I could feel the tension building already and I didn't want to wait. I brought my hips up higher to take him deeper and increase the pace. He released my nipple with a pop and brought his mouth back to mine. Our tongues matched with the pace that our bodies were setting and the next thing I knew stars were flashing behind my eyes. Two thrusts later and Chad was following me over the edge.

Unsure if I was awake or dreaming I ran my hand over his shaved hair feeling the prickles against my skin. The action caused his member to move inside me and I involuntarily moved against him. He moaned good naturedly, running his five o'clock shadow against my neck. I giggled and shifted again.

"Are you trying to kill me woman?"

"I apologize. We don't ever have to..." a hand quickly slapped over my mouth.

"Don't you dare say that," he gasped in mock horror.

I laughed at him as he got up and padded to the bathroom to clean up. He came back with a warm wet washcloth and a loving smile. While he wiped me clean the words he had said to me when we had first come home came crashing back to me. I couldn't very well say them back to him right at this moment given what had just happened. I didn't want him to think that I was only saying it because of the sex. I definitely wouldn't be. Once he had disposed of the towel, he pulled the covers down on the bed and we snuggled into the flannel sheets. Spooning, I quickly feel asleep cocooned in the warmth of the little cabin and the man that loved me.

Chapter 13

I woke up the next morning and stretched, expecting to find Chad's warm body next to mine. Instead I found an empty bed. I rolled over and slowly opened my eyes to peak at the clock, it read 7 o'clock, meaning I had a little time before my mother and stepfather showed up for brunch. Squelching down the panic that I had ruined a good thing by asking Chad to stay the night, I started to untangle myself from the sheets to head to the bathroom when I heard the water kick on in the shower.

My hopes perked up as I padded towards the sound. Chad's gym bag was on the floor with his dirty clothes beside it. I stripped off the t-shirt I had acquired at some point through the night and pulled back the curtain slightly to step in. He stood with his arms braced against the wall letting the hot water run down the back of his head and neck. I closed the curtain and stepped up behind him. Running my fingers from his hips to his shoulders gently, I felt his muscles dance beneath them and he let out a sigh.

"Trying to wash away your regrets?" I asked pressing a kiss between his shoulder blades.

Chad quickly turned around and pinned me to the wall with his arms on either side of my head. He was sporting a hard, throbbing erection that had my insides instantly heating at the thought. His eyes met mine and the need was evident.

"I don't have any regrets," he murmured, his lips a breath from mine. "Other than that I might have taken advantage of you in my anger with my sister."

I brought one of my hands up and stroked his hard-on from the tip down to his balls and back again. He let out a hiss and closed his eyes. I took this as a sign to keep going. So, this time I took charge. Keeping my hand on his member, I continued my ministrations while running a trail of kisses down his neck, across his collarbone, and down to one perky nipple. I took it in my mouth and sucked gently, nipping it lightly when Chad let out a low moan. I made my way across to the other side and repeated the process. My free hand drew circles on his stomach. Looking up I found him watching me with lust hazed eyes. I leaned up to kiss him and ran my hands up the length of his body to wrap around his neck.

Taking that as a hint his large hands came to my hips and around to grab my ass and lift. I wrapped my legs around him and felt the hard length of him flex against my core causing me to groan into his mouth. The sound spurred him to push my back up against the wall and create more friction between our lower bodies.

"I need you," I whispered panting, "now."

"We. Need. A. Condom."

He started to pull back enough to reach around to turn off the water, but I stopped him. I was on birth control and I was mid-cycle so I wasn't worried about pregnancy, and I knew Chad enough that I wasn't worried about disease of any kind. I pulled myself up on his body with my arms enough to cause the tip of his member to meet my entrance. Chad's eyes got wide and he looked at me questioningly.

"I'm on the pill," I told him quickly tightening my legs and loosening my hold a bit to take him in completely.

He moaned and I leaned my head back on the tile. It felt amazing. Pulling out slightly and pushing back in quicker he set the pace. It wasn't long before we were both pushed over the edge. My legs and arms shook with muscle fatigue and I struggled to hold on long enough for him to turn me around so that my back was to the warm water. Helping me down he washed me from head to toe and kissed me on the nose when he was done, before shutting off the water.

I opened the curtain and stepped out grabbing a towel to wrap myself in. I also wrapped up my hair while Chad was drying himself off. I couldn't take my eyes off him. His arm and leg muscles bunched and flexed as he worked the towel over his entire body. His blue eyes came up to meet mine and a knowing smile danced on his lips. Turning back towards the counter to grab my lotion for my face I blushed.

"Merry Christmas," he greeted coming over and planting a kiss on my shoulder before leaning down to get his boxer briefs from his bag.

"Merry Christmas," I responded applying the lotion and smiling at him in the mirror.

We finished getting ready for the day and I realized that this was how I wanted it to be every day. I didn't want to rush him, but I knew without a doubt that I wanted to ask him to move in with me and soon. Making our way into the living room, Chad went over to the stove to add wood and I made my way to the kitchen to start getting brunch ready.

"Can you stay?" I asked him while pulling eggs and milk from the refrigerator.

"Unfortunately no," he replied sitting to pull on his socks and boots.

I tried not to sulk, but I had really been looking forward to spending the day with him and my family together. I started the process of making scrambled eggs knowing my mother would be here sooner rather than later. While the eggs were warming in the pan, I went over and plugged in the tree. The white lights sparkling made my heart warm.

"I'll be back tonight," he told me getting up and crossing the room to me, "if that's okay."

"I would be hurt if you didn't." It was now or never. "How would you feel about staying here every night?"

His mouth dropped open and he appeared speechless. I started to back track mentally and I realized that I had definitely jumped the gun. For someone that had been scared to even start this relationship, here I was asking the guy to move in. It wasn't like we didn't know each other; we had been friends since we were kids.

"I'm sorry...." I stammered. "I know it's too quick. Forget I asked."

"I'm just surprised that's all," he stated finally finding his voice and tucking a stray piece of hair behind my ear. "I want nothing more than to wake up next to your beautiful face every morning. I love you."

"I love you too," I told him leaning up to brush a light kiss over his mouth. Just then I heard people stomping their boots off on the deck. My family had arrived.

The grin he gave me was priceless and was one that I would forever have etched in my mind. He gave me another quick kiss and moved to unlock the door letting my mom and Craig in. I helped my mother bring all the bags she was laden with into the kitchen while Craig stopped to chat with Chad as he dressed back up in warm layers. My mom took over the stove while I went back to give my man a final hug before he went out the door to clean up from the storm.

I couldn't contain my smile when I turned around from shutting the door behind him. Craig stood next to the tree unpacking some of the bags placing presents under it while my mom was busy bustling around the kitchen getting food ready. He stood up and motioned for me to come stand next to him. I did and he wrapped his arm around my shoulder kissing my hair.

"So glad to see our girl happy and in love," he told me squeezing gently.

"I didn't know I could be."

"You deserve it and Chad is a great man."

"I'm very lucky, that's for sure."

"And so is he," he said kissing my hair once again before releasing me to finish with the gifts.

Going into the kitchen to help my mom, I did the same thing Craig had done to me. I put my arm around her shoulder as she stood at the stove moving eggs around the pan and kissed her on the cheek. Despite my reservations about everything, I was so content and elated about Christmas. It felt so right to be with Chad and to have my parents here with me to celebrate the holiday. Nothing could ruin my little blissful bubble.

Finding the Way to Your Heart
Marcie Shumway

<u>Chapter 14</u>

A few hours later surrounded by wrapping paper and cuddled with my mom on the couch, my cup had runneth over. I couldn't remember a better Christmas since my father had passed away. My mom seemed just as content. The smile on her face was nonstop and her eyes were a little red from the happy tears she had just shed. Her and I had received roses, her a dozen and I a single, from Craig in honor of my father. It was something he had done for us quite frequently and was the reason I sported one on my hip permanently.

KNOCK! KNOCK!

I moved to get up and answer the door, knowing it wasn't Chad because he would have come right in. Craig waved me to sit down and answered the door himself. I heard a commotion and when I looked up he was letting my stepbrother, James, in the door along with his wife, Amy, and their son, Michael. My heart sank. Things had suddenly taken a turn I was not expecting.

"Merry Christmas ladies!" James boomed to us as he helped his wife and son strip off their jackets, hats, and boots.

"What are you doing here?!" my mom asked abandoning me on the couch to greet them.

"Well, we always spend Christmas together and it wouldn't be the same without you. We decided to take some extra time off from the dealership and come to you."

James and Amy co-owned a new and used car dealership. They also lived fairly close to my mother and

Craig, so I didn't understand why one holiday was such a big deal. It wasn't like we had a close relationship, for obvious reasons, so lord knows he wasn't here to see me.

Getting up from the couch I folded the blanket we had had wrapped around us and placed it over the back. To put some distance between James and myself I headed to the kitchen to make fresh coffee and to get together some of the leftover muffins and cookies. I needed to keep my hands busy, my brain was all over the place and I wasn't sure how to handle this, or their arrival.

Out of the corner of my eye I saw Michael come over and climb up on one of the bar stools by the island. He reached for a cookie and went back to the tablet he had in his hand. I poured him a glass of milk and received a small smile in return before his attention was diverted again. For a six-year-old he was quiet, too quiet, but then again his mother was too. Amy very rarely said a word and the last time I had seen her, she had served James his dinner and cleaned up behind him. She hadn't even eaten until he was completely doted on. Clearly his abuse hadn't ended with me.

I turned back around to pull out cups for the coffee and prepare a tray, the ever wonderful hostess. Listening to my mother and Craig gush over James and his growing business was raking my last nerve. I could feel myself start to shake with barely suppressed anxiety and anger. I had to remind myself that they didn't know what he had done all those years ago and that I had moved past the trauma. I had Chad now.

I felt something brush against my butt and assumed it was my nephew. Before I could turn a burly arm was thrown over my shoulders and a large body was tucked against my side. The smell of him alone had my stomach turning. I tried shrugging him off to move to the refrigerator for my mother's flavored creamer, but he held me steady. Unable to move I felt my last nerve crack.

"Get your arm off me," I hissed, low enough that the others couldn't hear.

"Well hello to you too, sister dear," he sneered without moving a muscle.

"I said. Get. Your. Arm. Off. Me," I repeated raising my voice, annunciating each word.

That's when I noticed everyone else had fallen silent. I turned slightly as James had finally moved his arm and our parents stood looking at us with wide eyes. Amy silently ushered Michael from his perch and into the bedroom, the door closing with a soft click. James had backed up to lean on the counter with his arms folded and a smirk on his face. I took a deep breath and closed my eyes.

"Lisa! How dare you be so rude! I taught you better manners than that!" my mother stammered, coming out of her shocked stupor.

"How dare I be so rude?" I replied. "How. Dare. I. Be. So. Rude?"

I could hear James chuckle behind me and I whipped around to put heated eyes on him. It didn't help and he didn't bother to hide his smile. He still thought I was weak and that I would never tell anyone about what had happened. James had always used his larger size against me, but I wasn't afraid of him anymore. Now I was just pissed.

"Mom," I said turning back around to look at her, "you have no clue what he did to me when I was a preteen."

"I know you guys argued, but all siblings do that," she stated waving it off like it wasn't a big deal.

"No, it was more than that."

I felt James take a step closer behind me and all the hairs went up on my neck. At the same time the front door opened and Chad stepped in. Knowing he was here gave me the strength I needed, if he didn't like what he heard I would be okay. It would finally be out in the open at least.

"He abused me from day one," I told them.

My mother shook her head in disbelief as Chad pulled off his winter gear and moved into the living room to stand behind my parents. Taking a couple of steps, I moved closer to them so I didn't have to yell. I wanted to hide it from Michael if at all possible.

"A little fighting is not abuse."

"I'm not talking about fighting. I'm talking about him coming into my room and taking advantage of me from the time I was ten until I was fourteen. I'm also talking about the fact that he threatened my life and yours if I ever told you."

The look on their faces when I finished had my heart in my throat. Craig and my mother looked back and forth between James and myself and looked like they honestly didn't believe me. Chad on the other hand had the controlled anger tick raging in his jaw and his hands were clenching and unclenching in fists by his sides. I'm pretty sure if I hadn't been standing between him and my stepbrother that he would have gone after him.

"That's impossible! We would have known!" my mother stuttered reaching for her husband, who's face had turned as white as a ghost.

James let out a breath behind me and a light chuckle only I could hear. I started to feel light headed and my heart broke with her words. They didn't believe me. Swiftly the walls started to feel like they were closing in around me. Darkness lined the edge of my vision and I put a hand out to steady myself before everything officially went black.

Chapter 15

"There we go," I heard a voice say softly, "come back to us, darlin'."

I opened my eyes and found Chad kneeling on the floor next to my couch holding an ice pack to my head. I didn't see or hear anyone else so I could only guess that they had either left or were outside. I immediately tried to sit up and was pushed back down gently as he shook his head.

"You took quite a bump to the head. Don't try to get up too fast," he told me gripping one of my hands with his free one.

"Where is everyone?" I asked in a whisper.

"Your family is gone," he told me with gritted teeth, "but JJ and Skye are here."

I closed my eyes and squeezed his hand as I felt a tear run down my cheek. Maybe if I had told them sooner. I couldn't be more grateful that Chad and my friends were still here. They were my true family, blood or not.

"It will be okay," I heard Skye whisper in my ear as she wiped my tears and took over holding the ice pack.

Her words and kindness just caused me to cry harder and my head to throb more than it already was. I wasn't sure if Christmas would ever be the same. Skye picked up my head and sat on the couch placing it gently back down in her small lap. I turned into her as much as I could with her growing belly and soaked up her strength. When I was able to control my crying I opened my eyes and brought my hand up to rub where Baby Hunter was actively kicking.

"He doesn't like it when my friend is upset any more than I do," she told me smoothing my hair back gently without touching the large egg shaped bump I could feel developing at my temple.

I rolled so I was on my back again, slowly sat up, and leaned against the back of the couch. Gradually opening my eyes, I saw Chad and JJ in the kitchen looking out the window above the sink talking in low voices. I couldn't hear what they were saying, but I could tell by the way they were standing that neither of them was happy.

"What happened?" I asked all three of them as I took the ice back from Skye and placed it against my head once more.

"Right after your mother basically told you that you were lying, you crumpled like a wet noddle knocking your head against the corner of the island. I tried to catch you, unfortunately I was too far away."

"And my family?"

"Your stepbrother dragged his family out of here like his butt was on fire. I had to force your mother and stepfather out."

"Did they say anything about what I said?"

"I'm sorry, baby," Chad apologized coming over and leaning on the back of my couch to cup my cheek. "They were in utter disbelief."

I leaned into him and closed my eyes for a second. When I opened them again they were all watching me with warm, caring eyes. I focused on Chad and covered his hand with one of mine.

"And you?"

"Of course I believe you," he stated. "It actually explains a lot."

"Why did you call Skye and JJ?"

"One because they are our friends and two because I knew that you and Skye had something in common," he admitted a bit sheepishly, "I thought it would make you feel better."

I pulled on his arm to bring him down to my level so that I could give him a quick kiss of thank you. It did actually make me feel better knowing Skye as there. She helped give me strength. I knew her battle and when I looked at her now it was amazing to see the transformation. It made me want to push to get through this.

"Can you please call my mother and ask them to come back? We need to talk about this."

Skye moved over to rub my back as I rested my head on the back of the couch. Chad grabbed my phone and did as I requested, but the tick in his jaw I had seen earlier had returned. JJ grabbed me a bottle of water and a couple of pain relievers to help with the insistent pounding in my head. A couple of the guys Chad and JJ played poker with weekly were EMT's so I was sure they had been in touch with them otherwise I would have been on my way to the hospital.

A half hour later I was snuggled against Chad's side, on the couch, when there was a knock on the door. Skye let my parents in as JJ continued to gather some snack like foods to go with the turkey soup that Karen had sent over for dinner. Craig sat down in the recliner and my mother sat on the end of the couch closest to him.

In the last few hours the two of them had aged. They both looked awful, exhausted and drawn. Clearly they were battling with what I told them. I was relieved and glad it was out in the open, especially after all these years, yet at the same time I hated the effect it was having on these people that had done everything they possibly could to raise us right.

"I'm sorry I dropped the ball on you that way," I told them not moving from where I was laying.

"We just have a hard time with the fact that this happened under our roof and that we weren't even aware of it," Craig said hesitantly.

"I learned early on to be quiet when he came into my room. I was scared and he threatened my life and my mother's more times than I could count."

Craig sat shaking his head, his face still pale. My mother was stoic and mute. I could see the tears in her eyes, however she hadn't made a move towards me. Chad ran his hand up and down my arm in comfort, while JJ and Skye brought out food and placed it on the coffee table for everyone along with tea and coffee. I shot them each a smile.

"Why would he do that, he loves your mother," my stepfather argued.

"It had nothing to do with my mom," I informed him sitting up straighter, very gingerly. "He used it to keep me quiet because he knew what he was doing was wrong."

Skye and JJ sat down at the kitchen table and ate, keeping near enough that they could hear and be there if I needed them. Chad sat up once I was no longer leaning on him and grabbed a mug of soup to place in my hands along with a muffin. I took a sip of the warm liquid and a bite of the muffin before looking up at them again.

My mother watched me with worried eyes. Her concern for me as her child was battling with the skepticism of my story. Craig shook his head off and on. Suddenly I saw his eyes go wide and he looked up at me sharply. I stopped with my cup midway to my mouth and questioned him with my eyes.

"Oh my god!" he exclaimed jumping up and running out the door.

I could hear Craig retching outside. Obviously something had dawned on him and he couldn't handle it. I motioned for Chad to go out and check on him as my mother stared after him in shock. I finished my dinner just as they came back in and Chad came over to sit back where he had been, leaning his arm around the back of the couch behind me. I could hear Skye and JJ cleaning up since my mother and Craig had both waived off food after each taking a cup of coffee.

"It's true, isn't it? That's why you would never let him hug you or touch you, why you started dressing provocatively, why you never had a steady boyfriend?" Craig asked putting his elbows on his knees with the coffee cup loosely in his hands.

My mom gasped as I nodded slightly and put her hand over her mouth. The waterworks finally let loose and she came over to the couch on the other side of me and delicately pulled me into her arms. Her sobbing and murmured apologies had tears forming in my eyes. With my head pounding I tried not to cry hard because I knew it would just make it worse. Craig finally came over and kneeled by the couch, placing himself so that he was hugging both of us.

I'm not sure how long we stayed that way. When we finally separated Skye handed us all tissues and Chad pulled me towards him to touch an ice pack softly to my head once again. I leaned into his touch. I felt spent emotionally and physically. A load had been lifted, but I knew this was only the beginning of the journey to truly get over the abuse.

An hour later my parents, JJ and Skye left leaving just Chad and I. He tucked me into bed and I could hear him go back out into the living room to stoke the fire one final time and to lock up for the night. I dozed lightly until I felt him crawl into bed beside me. He pulled me against his side and I put my head on his chest.

Fighting sleep, I couldn't help but think how lucky I was to have this amazing man by my side through this whole thing. Most would have run at the first admission. I felt his lips brush against my forehead and heard him whisper 'I love you'. Smiling I drifted off into a deep sleep for the first time in years.

Chapter 16

A few days later my head was finally feeling better, but my heart and emotions were stretched thin. My stepbrother had not fled town as I had hoped, instead he and his family were sticking around until New Years. He used the excuse of wanting a vacation with his entire family, however James was using every opportunity to try to turn the tables on me after the confession. This left my poor mother and stepfather feeling torn and run ragged. As much as I wanted to spend time with them, I tried to let them be so there wasn't any added pressure on them.

JJ informed me that I didn't need to go back to work, and to take some time off, however I needed the distraction. I couldn't convince Chad though that I could drive myself. I had to admit the loving attention he showered on me was pretty great, though a little hard to get used to.

"You ready to go?" Chad asked popping his head through the door way to my office.

"I'm sorry, Mr. Kendall," I apologized putting my finger up to Chad to signal one minute.

"The delivery was late due to the storm, but the guys have the sled in the shop now and it should be ready by tomorrow or New Year's Eve at the latest."

I saw Chad leaning on the doorframe shaking his head as I sweet talked the customer a little more before hanging up. I smiled at him as I logged off my computer and grabbed my work bag. Putting my jacket on I made my way over to him as he continued to smirk and shake his head. I raised my eyebrow at him in question as I came to a stop inches from him.

"You know, if I wasn't comfortable in the fact that I was your boyfriend and that you loved me, I would be worried that you were going to run off with Earle," he told me putting his hands on my hips and pulling me flush against him.

"Who's to say I still wouldn't?" I teased leaning in close enough to feel his breath against my lips.

That was all the invitation he needed. Chad's lips were forceful enough to have me gasping and he used the opportunity to put his tongue in my mouth to duel with mine. I sucked once gently and changed the angle to take the kiss deeper. With all the craziness the past few days I had missed our banter and the sexual charge that seemed to come so easy to us.

"Gross! Really guys?" I heard JJ's voice tease through my Chad induced haze.

I felt his lips smile under mine as he gave me one more chaste kiss before pulling away. We followed JJ to the front door and stood with him as he closed up for the night, since we were the last ones out. It was nice to get back into the routine of my everyday life and definitely helped to settle my nerves a bit. The joking and the ease between the men also warmed my soul.

"You're coming to poker tonight, right?" JJ asked, poised to get into his truck.

"Yes, he is," I answered before Chad could turn him down.

I waved JJ off before my boyfriend could disagree. He was laughing as he pulled away from us to make the short trek to his house. I'm glad someone was because I could already see the argument brewing within Chad. He hadn't exactly left my side much lately, not that I was complaining, but a girl could use some breathing room and I knew he needed his time with JJ.

"I'm not going," he informed me as we buckled up and he started the truck.

"I'm a grown-up," I told him turning in my seat slightly to look at him. "I don't need a baby-sitter."

I saw his face harden and fall all at the same time. I hadn't meant to sound ungrateful or mean, yet I had always been independent and the last few days had left me feeling overwhelmed. I knew that he loved me and was only trying to protect me. I leaned over the center console and gently tugged on his forearm to get him to release his grip on the steering wheel. When he finally gave I intertwined my fingers with his and rubbed my other hand up and down his arm. He still wouldn't look at me and his face was rigid.

Pulling into my driveway, he pulled to stop in front of the garage and turned off the truck. The silence was eerie. I had never seen Chad this upset before. He continued to look forward and I could see that his jaw was clenched. I reached over with my free hand and pulled his chin so that he was looking at me. The hurt in his eyes took my breath away.

"I know you love me and you want what's best for me," I started, treading lightly, "but I also want this to be a relationship where we enjoy each other as well as our own lives."

I saw his understanding immediately, however the look he had didn't change. His eyes held mine. I ran my hand up his face to cup his cheek and he turned his head slightly to kiss my palm, never breaking eye contact.

"I know I hold on too tight," he said in a low voice. "Now that I have you I don't want to let you go."

I smiled and leaned over more to kiss him sweetly. Words like those weren't just words coming from this man, that I knew. It made me want to work harder to get past all this drama in my life to be with him and be happy.

"I'm not going anywhere. Your friends are missing you and getting a little jealous though."

"Fine, I'll go," he affirmed squeezing my fingers in the hands that we had sitting on the center console. "Expect me back early though and you'd better be ready to be woken up."

I laughed and gave him a quick kiss before hoping out on my own and waving to him as he started the truck and backed out. I unlocked the door and went inside. It was quiet, it was nice. I bustled around to clean up what little mess there was now that the Christmas decorations had been taken down and the tree removed.

Finally able to settle down, I changed into a tank top and yoga pants. Curling up on the couch with a pint of ice cream I put on one of my Hallmark movies and settled in. As the movie was finishing a couple hours later I found that I was having a hard time keeping my eyes open. I was kind of bummed. I was hoping for some more time to enjoy my evening, but clearly my body was telling me otherwise.

I locked up the front door and stocked the woodstove before heading to the bedroom. I plugged my phone in and set it on an app playing soft country music. Crawling into bed without Chad felt weird, but I didn't think about it long before the warmth of being under the covers pulled me under.

I woke up some time later to the bed dipping on one side from human weight. I peeked up at the alarm clock and was surprised when it only read 8:30. I obviously hadn't been asleep long and Chad was home earlier than I thought he would be. I stretched and rolled over to be closer to him. That's when I got a whiff of cologne. Cologne that wasn't his and that took me back to being ten years old again.

I tried not to panic and started to move slowly so as not to grab his attention. It was too late. Before I could move James whipped back the covers and straddled me with his beefy body. One of his hands held my hands above my head while the other ran down my body to the hem of my shirt. His lips were inches from mine and I could smell alcohol on his breath.

"You thought they would believe you all these years later," he hissed forcing a kiss on my lips. "Now it's time for your punishment."

The second time he tried to kiss me I bit down on his lower lip as hard as I could and pulled to break my hands free. Able to do so in his moment of pain, I shoved at him as hard as I could. He wouldn't budge, but he was still wrapped up in his bleeding lip so I wiggled up as far as I could and quickly brought my knee up to connect with his groin. That was enough to send him rolling off me and I scrambled up.

I thought I could make it to the bathroom and lock myself in until Chad came home. Turning when I came off the bed, strong arms caught me by the waist stopping me and hauled me against a solid body. I brought my heel down on his instep, however this time he just hissed without letting go.

"We aren't done yet," he whispered loudly in my ear.

"Oh. Yes. You. Are." Came a clipped voice from the door.

I wanted to breathe a sigh of relief. The grip around my hips tightened from one arm while the other came up to wrap around my throat. He turned us slowly and found both Chad and JJ standing in the doorway. This was not looking good. Chad stood in front of his friend and his hands were flexing in and out of fists, much like Christmas Day. Only this time, I wasn't going to be able to hold him back once he got his hands on James.

"This has nothing to do with you," James told him calmly, "this is between my little sister and me."

"It has everything to do with me," Chad retorted coming a step closer. "That woman is mine and after years she has finally let me in. You are not going to get in the way of that."

I felt my stepbrother stiffen against me and the arm against my throat tighten a notch. I felt my airway constricting and started to see darkness on the edges of my eye line. I refused to pass out again because of this man, but then I remembered something that someone had told me. If I pretended to pass out and shifted my deadweight forward it would set him off balance. This was the only way I could think of to get him to let me go and allow JJ and Chad the chance to get a handle on him before the cops could arrive.

Taking a deep breath, I dumped all my weight forward and slumped in his arms. The shift in position and weight threw him off enough that he released the hand against my throat and stumbled. I thanked the gods at that moment that he was slightly inebriated, otherwise it might not have worked. I bent over at the waist and put my hands out as I saw the floor coming closer. Before I knew what was happening a fist came buzzing by me and I heard the sickening sound of it connecting with flesh. James' remaining arm let go and I tumbled to the floor.

JJ's strong arms came around me and dragged me from the room. Helping me to my feet he pulled me towards the garage. I hesitated when I heard the sounds coming from the bedroom. Nauseating sounds of bone on bone and flesh smacking flesh filled the air. I looked at JJ with wide eyes. I didn't want Chad and James to kill each other and I knew if JJ didn't go back in there that would happen. He ushered me into the garage and handed me his cell phone as he got ready to shut the door behind me.

"The cops are already on their way. We called them when we saw his car parked down the road. Call Skye and stay put until I come back to get you."

I tucked myself in the corner by the front of my Jeep and texted Skye that we had a situation. I didn't want to call her because I was trying to listen for sirens, and to what was going on inside the house. It wasn't long before I heard them and the SUVs of the state police skidding to a halt in my driveway. I heard their boots on the deck and then in the house. I put my head on my knees and my arms around them. Every part of my body was shaking uncontrollably.

Suddenly the lights turned on in the garage and I felt a presence by my side. I sniffed to see if I could smell the cologne before I opened my eyes and lifted my head.

JJ was crouched down next to me and he rested one hand on my shoulder. He looked no worse for wear other than his clothes being a little rumpled and his shirt ripped under his jacket. He helped me stand and circled me in his arms when I was able to get my feet under me.

JJ helped me into the house and once we were there I started shaking again. Cops were everywhere and Skye was just coming in the front door. She started to reach for me, but I wanted Chad I needed to know he was okay. I looked towards the kitchen and there he sat with a paramedic we knew. Blood was dripping down his face from a cut above his brow, and one eye was already starting to turn purple and swell.

I rushed to him before anyone could stop me and crumpled at his feet. I heard him mutter something to the guy working on his head wound and then I felt his hands pick me up under my arm pits. I tried to help him, however my legs were jelly. I curled into his lap once he had pulled me up enough and put my head where I could listen to his heart beating, strong and true.

"I'm fine," he whispered. "He got in a couple of lucky shots that's all."

Knowing he was okay and hearing the steady 'thump, thump' in my ear, calmed me down. Looking up and seeing Skye fussing over JJ, and knowing he was fine as well also helped ease my fears. When my mom came bursting through the door with Craig hot on her heels, I had had enough. The blackness that had threatened me earlier on in the night finally closed in.

Chapter 17

Sitting at the Conrad's large dining room table surrounded by those I loved, and many that were still renting cabins, I couldn't be happier to be ringing in the New Year with everyone. I looked around and took everything in as we ate. Our friends Kyle and Sam were here and Sam was gushing over how much Skye had changed since she saw her last, while Kyle was talking to JJ about a repair he needed done on his lawnmower in the spring. Chad was chatting with his dad about some things that needed to be done on a cabin, and his mother was telling my mother some sort of gossip that had them giggling like little girls.

My stepfather was quiet, as he had been since my stepbrother's arrest, but he smiled as our eyes connected. When I turned to take a sip from my wine glass I found Morgan watching me. The two of us hadn't seen each other, never mind talked, since the Christmas Eve party. I knew Chad was still upset with her and I broke my gaze from her when I felt his hand on my thigh. I covered it with one of my own.

"You okay?" he whispered in my ear as I took a bite of the pork roast on my plate.

"I'm good, I promise," I told him smiling at him as I took in the black eye he sported and the six stitches above his right brow.

He leaned in and kissed my nose before being pulled into another conversation with his father. Duncan was vibrant as ever and truly loved having everyone gathered in his home. All the campers enjoyed being included in the holiday events and were talking animatedly amongst themselves.

When we finished eating I offered to help Morgan and Karen clean up again, much like I had on Christmas Eve. I waved Chad off when he tried to follow me into the kitchen. I was the first one in so I worked on filling the large sink with soap and hot water for the items that couldn't be put in the dishwasher. I saw an arm drop in a serving platter and was surprised when I looked up and saw Morgan. She leaned past me and turned off the water.

"I wanted to apologize for Christmas Eve. I may have been a little overprotective of my big brother," she confessed leaning against the large island.

"I wouldn't expect any less, Morgan," I admitted honestly. "

"I know, but I overstepped my bounds that night. I shouldn't have said or thought some of the things I did."

"Don't worry about it," I told her placing my hand on her arm. "I know what people thought of me."

"It doesn't make it right though!" she exclaimed with tears in her eyes as she covered my hand with one of her own.

Karen came in and I locked eyes with her. When she saw that Morgan and I were in the middle of something, she stopped. I smiled at her and motioned my head for her to go back to the dining room and give us a minute. She nodded in understanding and blew me a kiss on her way back out.

"It's isn't right," I agreed. "Those that know me know why I was that way and I am working on being a better person."

"You are a beautiful, amazing, and strong woman and my brother is very lucky to have you," she gushed taking both of my hands in hers. "I see how much you care about him and how happy he is. That's all that matters to me."

I pulled my hands from hers and hugged her tightly. Before I released her, her brother came in, hands full of dishes. I let Morgan go and took them from him, motioning for him to talk to his sister. As I put the dishes in the water and started it running again to finish filling the sink, I could hear them talking in muted tones behind me. I heard the door open and turned to see Karen coming in, and Chad embracing his sister and kissing the top of her head.

I smiled at the scene and took the dishes Karen held in her hands. The smile that graced her face at the reunion of her children was enough to have me ushering them all out of the kitchen while I finished the cleanup. Skye and Sam appeared to help me and before we were done the three of us were laughing together like we had in high school. It felt great.

When we went back to the living room games were fully underway. Each corner had a different board game and those that weren't playing were milling about with drinks in hand. Chad, JJ, Kyle, and one of the male campers were all engrossed in a humorous game of Pictionary that had the three of us ladies sitting down to watch. I don't think I had laughed that long or hard in a long time. By the time the game was over my stomach muscles felt like I had just done an extreme workout at the gym.

A few hours later, midnight was fast approaching and I offered to get the bottles of champagne and sparkling cider needed to ring in the New Year. Grabbing a basket from the pantry I opened the door to the commercial grade refrigerator and started to fill it. On my last trip to turn around I connected with a solid chest and warm arms.

"I'm missing my lady tonight and you've been in the same room," Chad murmured in my ear, leaving a trail of butterfly kisses down my neck.

"I know, I've missed you too," I replied angling my neck to give him better access as I shifted the bottles in my hands.

"We will continue this later," he huffed teasingly, kissing me on the lips as he took the last of the bottles from my hands so I could shut the refrigerator door.

Taking the full basket in one hand and my hand in the other we made our way to the living room where everyone was ready with their glasses. Karen and Duncan had the large flat screen set to watch the ball drop and the anticipation was growing. Each couple had paired off ready to celebrate with those they loved. Even Kyle and Sam looked happy and content, unlike the other times I had seen them recently.

The picture changed and the countdown began. Chad turned me and looked me in the eyes as the numbers slowly started to trickle down. It was like we were the only two in the room. THREE! This was how I always wanted to ring in the New Year. TWO! With this man by my side and in my heart. ONE! Kissing me as though I was all he ever needed and wanted. HAPPY NEW YEAR!

<u>Chapter 18</u>

I woke up a few days later to a draft across my belly and hip. Opening my eyes, I found that Chad had pulled my shirt up and my shorts down enough to see my tattoo. He was running his fingers lightly across the design. It wasn't as though he had never seen it before, after all he had gone with me to get mine, and had ended up with his.

"Is there a problem?" I asked, putting my hands under my head to prop myself up to look at him.

"Did you know that I fell in love with you the day you asked me to go get this with you?"

I shook my head as I felt tears prickling the backs of my eyes. I pulled one of my hands out from behind my head and traced it over the tattoo decorating his shoulder and arm.

"I couldn't believe that you had asked me, out of all your friends, you asked me."

"Did you know that I fell in love with you that very same day because you put a piece of my tattoo on your arm?"

His smile and the sparkle in his eye could have blinded a room. He leaned over and dropped a kiss on my rose before covering me back up, that's when I noticed that he had showered and already had his jeans on. So much for a relaxing morning in bed.

"Where are you going?" I moaned rolling over feigning laziness.

"My dad called and wants to get started on that cabin," Chad said chuckling and pulling on a long sleeved t-shirt. "I guess mom has it rented for next week."

I climbed out of bed as he finished getting ready. I cleaned up and put on comfortable clothes. Padding out to the kitchen, I had just started a cup of coffee as Chad came out and stoked the fire for me. I knew he wanted to get going so I grabbed one of his favorite breakfast burritos for him and warmed it in the microwave.

While he layered up, I put his coffee into a travel mug and wrapped his burrito in a paper towel. Since he already had his boots on I brought everything over to him. He smiled in thank you, taking the food and handle of the mug in one hand, so he could use the other to cup the back of my neck and bring me in for a long, slow, deep kiss.

"You know, you make it really hard not to drag you back to the bedroom," I told him, bracing myself against his chest with my hands.

"I know, but it has to last all day," he exaggerated using his arms.

"Cause you've never done it before," I teased rolling my eyes and stepping away.

"Eh. It's different now," he retorted as he reached out to slap my butt playfully as I pulled from his reach. "You going to be all set with your mom and Craig today?"

"Yep. They are bringing over breakfast from The Pit and are going to hit the road as soon as we're done."

Once I assured him everything would be fine, he headed out the door. I did a quick inspection of the cabin and when I was satisfied all was in order I went back to the kitchen to get coffee ready for the three of us. I had just pulled the handle down to start the first cup when I heard a short beep signaling that they had arrived. I grabbed my mom's preferred coffee creamer from the refrigerator and my stepfather's sugar packets from a drawer in the island and set them on the kitchen table. Seconds later both of them came traipsing through the door with bags in their hands and pink cheeks from the cold.

"Need help?" I asked reaching back in the refrigerator for the juice.

"All set," Craig replied setting his and my mother's bags down before returning to help her with her coat, and to pull off his own.

I continued setting the table and swapped out the cup that was ready to start another. When they had finished getting off their winter garb they proceeded to unpack the bags. By the time they had the bags cleared off the table and were ready to eat I had all the coffee cups done. They had brought me French Toast made with Texas Toast and a large side order of bacon and home fries. My mouth watered from the smell as I sat down to dig in.

"So are you guys excited to get on the road and get home?" I asked with my mouth partially full.

"Didn't I teach you any manners?" my mom asked jokingly as she also talked over a mouth half full of food.

"Kinda," Craig answered my original question truthfully sharing a look with my mother.

It was one of those looks that said something was coming. That they had some big news to share. I stopped chewing and swallowed, staring at them. I took a swig of juice and waited for them to tell me what was on their minds.

"Just tell me," I told them before attempting to eat any more.

"Well, we were thinking about moving back to Maine," my mother told me with a small smile.

I could see the nervousness behind her admission. They kept exchanging looks and my stepfather had gripped her hand where it was sitting on the table. My stomach felt like it had a steel ball sitting in it. I didn't know if I could take having them that close. Granted we were working on our relationship, but I couldn't take my mother constantly over my shoulder.

"Oh, but not in Birch Wood!" she rushed to tell me when she saw the panic that I couldn't hide, flitter across my face.

"Where are you thinking then?" I asked tentatively.

"Oh probably some place like Pike or Allen Town. More city than country."

I let out a sigh of relief. Both places were at least an hour away, yet still much closer than they had been in Massachusetts. That did make me happy. I hadn't realized how much I had missed them despite the weight of the secret.

"We don't want to invade your life," my stepfather reassured me. "However, with everything that has happened we want to live closer and be a bigger part of your it."

"That sounds perfect," I told them resting my hand on top of their joined ones.

I saw them both release the breaths they had been holding. I hadn't realized that they had been so nervous about my reaction and thoughts about their move. That's when my mind went to Amy. I hadn't heard anything about her or Michael since James had been arrested. How was she going to handle the business and their home alone?

"What about Amy and Michael?"

"Unfortunately we can't control her and what she decides to do. We will support her in any way that we can," my mom told me as she got up to make another cup of coffee.

"We offered to help her sell the business and their house and to have them temporarily move in with us until she decided exactly what she was going to do. She thanked us profusely, yet declined," Craig told me as he handed my mother his cup and mine to refill as well.

"I'm sure she is still processing. I don't think she saw any of this coming," I murmured. "I know he has abused them in some way, shape, or form, but I don't think that she had any clue of what he did to me."

"None of us did," Craig said sadly, putting his hand over mine and squeezing it gently. "I'm sorry that you had to go through that and that you felt you had to carry that secret alone for so long."

"It is part of who I am at this point and honestly has made me a stronger person. It has also led me to Chad and who knows if I would have ended up with him if I hadn't been through what I had. I also wouldn't have had the chance to work on my relationship with you guys," I informed him squeezing back and flashing my mother a loving smile. "I love you both so much."

"Ditto, love. Ditto."

Chapter 19

The beginning of March dawned unseasonably warm and the ground was fairly clear of snow. The early storms of the winter had tapered off leaving us with below average snowfall totals for the year and had the end of the season feeling more like late spring. I couldn't have been more grateful as it gave me a chance to get out and do some running on the roads rather than being cooped up in the gym.

As I finished my last leg and made it into the driveway I noticed that Chad's truck was already running. Some mornings he would join me while others he would wait for me to come back and we would have breakfast together before we both headed out to work. Skye's due date was nearing and I wondered if his truck running meant that she was at the hospital. Kicking it up a notch I made it to the porch quicker than I should have with a cool down and threw open the door.

"Skye? Is she in labor?" I asked breathlessly as I stormed into the house to find Chad putting coffee in two travel mugs.

"Nope, I have a surprise for you though, so go change your clothes," came the reply with a chuckle.

Slipping off my shoes I let out a sigh of relief mixed with disappointment. I was so excited to see Skye and JJ's baby. I know she had been getting more and more uncomfortable and her belly had definitely dropped causing her to waddle a bit. It was the cutest thing. I ran to the bedroom and exchanged my workout clothes for jeans, a long sleeved t-shirt, a hooded sweatshirt, and wool socks.

When I came out Chad was standing by the door with our coffees and my jacket in hand. I put on and laced my hiking boots in record time while pulling on my jacket and grabbing my coffee mug. I wasn't normally a surprise person, however, my man looked so excited and his smile was ear to ear so it rubbed off on me. He grabbed my hand and laced his fingers through mine as he tugged me out the door and to his truck.

I climbed in and laughed as he shut the door quickly behind me and ran around the front of the vehicle to his side. He winked at me as he jumped in and buckled up causing me to giggle. Oh how I loved this man. No one made me laugh like he did.

"So, any hints?" I asked as we pulled out of the driveway.

"Nope, you will just have to wait and see."

I smiled from behind my cup and left him alone. His face was still lit up and he sipped from his cup as well. We drove towards Conrad's Cabins & Lodge and I was taken back when he pulled over just past his parent's property at a dirt road that had a chain across it a truck length in. He hopped out and removed the chain. When he got back into the truck I looked at him with my eyebrows raised, and he just laughed.

Driving slowly due to the soft ground we wound our way down a long road, or what I thought was a road until a house with a large two bay garage came into view. Again I looked over at Chad, but other than the smile he gave away no hints. Looking back at the house I noticed that it was a new construction. The ground work around it was still in progress.

"Chad?"

He put the truck in park and hopped out. Coming around to my side he opened my door and pulled me from my seat and into his arms. Carrying me newlywed style he set my feet down on the beautiful farmer's porch and opened the door pushing it slightly so I could walk in ahead of him. Cardboard trails lined the floors, obviously the hardwood floors were done and other work was still being finished up.

Downstairs was a semi-open plan with kitchen, dining room, and living room all connected. The master bedroom and bathroom were also on the first floor and I almost died when I saw the jetted tub and enormous standing shower stall. After I was done drooling Chad pointed up the stairs, so I went up and found two bedrooms and another full bath. It was set up exactly how I wanted my house to be. Coming down the stairs I again questioned him with my eyes with no response. He reached for my hand and I gave it to him. Again he intertwined my fingers with his and tugged me to the back of the house and out the large French doors in the kitchen.

That's when I noticed it. In a tree at the back of the cleared property was a tree stand and from it hung a hat. It looked identical to Chad's tattoo. Looking down the tree I saw a single rose and a small box. He stopped us just in front of the tree and turned to look at me. I could only hope he was doing what I thought he was and tears instantly welled up in my eyes.

"Lisa, I know we haven't been together all that long officially, but I have loved you for years. I want to spend the rest of my life by your side day in and day out, laughing with you and fighting with you, and making a family with you. Please come live in this house with me, be my wife, and be the mother of my children."

I couldn't have answered him if I wanted to. I nodded as I sobbed uncontrollably and put my left hand out for him to slide the ring on. It was a beautiful setting with one diamond lifted up between two smaller ones and three down each side of the band. He stood and gathered me in his arms as he kissed my forehead, my lips, and my neck. I tried to see my hand through the tears and around his head. When I could finally see I laughed with joy.

I had never thought I would find someone that loved me the way this man did or that I even deserved it. Nor did I ever think I could love someone as much as I loved him. Life had definitely taken an unexpected yet amazing turn. Who would have guessed that releasing those pent up secrets could help you find the way to your heart?

Finding the Way to Your Heart
Marcie Shumway

Finding the Way to Your Heart
Marcie Shumway

Finding the Way to Your Heart
Marcie Shumway

Finding the Way to Your Heart
Marcie Shumway

Finding the Way to Your Heart
Marcie Shumway

Finding the Way to Your Heart
Marcie Shumway

Finding the Way to Your Heart
Marcie Shumway

Finding the Way to Your Heart
Marcie Shumway

Finding the Way to Your Heart
Marcie Shumway

Finding the Way to Your Heart
Marcie Shumway

Finding the Way to Your Heart
Marcie Shumway

Finding the Way to Your Heart
Marcie Shumway

www.ingramcontent.com/pod-product-compliance
Lightning Source LLC
Chambersburg PA
CBHW070456130626
46555CB00003B/1027